GHOST OF A CHANCE

Don't miss these other great books by Lauren Barnholdt:

Girl Meets Ghost

Book 1: *Girl Meets Ghost*

Book 2: *The Harder the Fall*

Fake Me a Match

Rules for Secret Keeping

The Secret Identity of Devon Delaney

Devon Delaney Should Totally Know Better

Four Truths and a Lie

GIRL MEETS GHOST

GHOST OF A CHANCE

LAUREN BARNHOLDT

Aladdin
NEW YORK LONDON TORONTO SYDNEY NEW DELHI

An imprint of Simon & Schuster Children's Publishing Division
1230 Avenue of the Americas, New York, NY 10020
First Aladdin paperback edition October 2014

Also available in an Aladdin hardcover edition.
For information about special discounts for bulk purchases,
please contact Simon & Schuster Special Sales at 1-866-506-1949
or business@simonandschuster.com.
The Simon & Schuster Speakers Bureau can bring authors to your live event.
For more information or to book an event contact the Simon & Schuster Speakers
Bureau at 1-866-248-3049 or visit our website at www.simonspeakers.com.
Series design by Lisa Vega
Cover design by Jeanine Henderson
The text of this book was set in Minion.
Manufactured in the United States of America 0914 OFF
10 9 8 7 6 5 4 3 2 1
The Library of Congress has cataloged the hardcover edition as follows:
Barnholdt, Lauren.
Ghost of a chance / by Lauren Barnholdt. — First Aladdin hardcover edition.
p. cm. — (Girl meets ghost ; #3)
Summary: After learning that she can see ghosts, twelve-year-old Kendall's disbelieving boyfriend breaks up with her.
[1. Ghosts—Fiction. 2. Psychic ability—Fiction. 3. Dating (Social customs)—Fiction.]
I. Title.
PZ7.B2667Gh 2014
[Fic]—dc23
2013025497
ISBN 978-1-4424-4248-1 (hc)
ISBN 978-1-4424-2148-6 (pbk)
ISBN 978-1-4424-2151-6 (eBook)

GHOST OF A CHANCE

Chapter 1

This definitely might be the most horrible idea I've ever had. Like, *ever*. And let's face it, I've had some pretty horrible ideas. I mean, my life is kind of a mess right now.

Case in point:

1. I've told the maybe love of my life, Brandon Dunham, that I can see ghosts. Yes, it's true that I can see ghosts, but why, why, why would I tell him that? Am I crazy? What *good* did I think could possibly come of it? Especially since one of the ghosts I can see is his mom.

2. After I told Brandon about the whole seeing-ghosts thing, he accused me of lying, and then he left me sitting in the snack bar of the YMCA. Which I'm pretty sure means we've broken up.

3. After he left, I decided I should go see my mom. Now, I know what you're thinking—why is going to see your mom on a list of things that have turned your life into a big horrible disaster, Kendall? If I were a normal girl with a normal relationship with my mom, going to see her wouldn't be on this list. But I'm not a normal girl. And I don't have a normal relationship with my mother. I see ghosts. And I haven't seen my mom since I was a baby.

Anyway, the reason I had no choice but to go see my mom is because the ghost of Brandon Dunham's mom keeps showing up and threatening me, and then I found out that *my* mom and Mrs. Dunham were best friends when they were younger. So I had to come see my mom so I could ask her if she has any idea why the heck Mrs. Dunham won't leave me alone.

And now here I am, following my mom down the front hallway of her house. A house I've never been to. A house I've never even *seen*. So. Weird.

"Do you want some tea or something?" she asks as we walk into the kitchen. She opens the fridge and looks inside. "I didn't know you were coming. Otherwise I would have picked up some food. . . ."

"Tea would be great," I say. I don't really like tea, but whatever. I mean, we need to have something to do, don't we? We can't just be sitting here, having what is sure to be an awkward conversation, without something to eat or drink.

"Go ahead, have a seat," my mom says.

I slide my arms out of my coat and drape it across the back of a kitchen chair. It's a nice house, I decide. It looks big from the outside, but inside it feels cozy and warm. There are green-and-white-striped place mats on the table, and the chairs are the kind with cushions on them.

The chairs in my kitchen at home don't have cushions. In fact, now that I think about it, the chairs at my house are extremely uncomfortable. They force you to sit ramrod straight. I've never really thought about it before, but now I wonder, if my mom had been living with us this whole time, would she have made sure we always had comfy chairs?

"Here you go," she says, putting a mug of tea down in front of me.

"Thanks." I take a sip. It's so hot that it burns my tongue.

There's an awkward pause, and I really can't even look at her, because it's way too weird. I mean, what am I supposed to say? What am I supposed to do? The silence stretches on for another moment.

"I like your house," I say.

"Thank you."

"You're welcome." I swallow and feel emotions swirling through me. I want to ask her the question I've always wondered, the only thing I really want to know about her life. "Do you . . . Are you . . . I mean, do you live here alone?"

She nods.

"You're not married?"

She shakes her head.

"And you don't have any kids? I mean, uh, besides me."

"No." She's looking right at me as she says it. I let go of the breath I've been holding and feel the tightness in my chest loosen just a little. I don't want to know anything else about my mom, about her life, about what she does for a living or whether or not she's happy. She doesn't deserve my curiosity.

But I had to know if she had a new family. If she did, I don't think I'd ever be able to forgive her. For her to have left me is bad enough—but for her to have left me and then started another family would be much worse.

There's another short silence, like maybe she's waiting for me to ask her more questions about her life. But there's no way I'm going to do that. I didn't come here to find out about her. I came here for answers.

"Kendall," she says finally, wrapping her hands around the mug in front of her. "I know why you're here."

"You do?"

She nods and then sighs. "I'm sure you have a lot of questions. But you need to know that I may not be able to answer all of them."

"What do you mean?" I pick up my cup of tea, blow on it, and take another sip.

"What I mean is that there might be some things that you have to figure out on your own."

I bite back a laugh. It's kind of hilarious that she's saying that, since I've had to figure out things on my own for pretty much my whole life. Like how to talk to boys, how to put on makeup, how to dress, how to pretty much do everything girls need to know that their dads can't teach them.

"Yeah, well, wouldn't be the first time," I mutter under my breath. It's completely petty and immature to mutter under your breath, but I'm in a petty and immature kind of mood.

She opens her mouth to say something, but then thinks better of it. "That's fair."

Which just makes it worse, because at least if she was making excuses and trying to justify the fact that she left when I was little, I could blame her and yell at her. But her saying it's fair takes the wind out of my sails.

Okay, Kendall, I tell myself. *You need to take control of this situation.* This isn't one of those sappy reality TV shows where someone is looking for their long-lost relative, and then, once they find them, they start working on repairing their relationship. (Even though I totally love those shows. Honestly, who doesn't? They always have happy endings, which is completely the opposite of real life. Even though they call them reality TV shows, which is kind of ridiculous.)

"Look," I say, sitting up straight in my chair and looking my mom right in the eye. "I didn't come here for some kind of big reunion scene. I came here because I need to know about you and Julie Dunham."

She nods, like she expected this. Which makes no sense. How can she know I would show up wanting to know about Brandon's mom? Unless my dad called her and told her I was asking him questions about Julie Dunham.

Ohmigod. That must be it! My dad and my mom have been talking behind my back! It makes sense. Think about it. My dad had a girlfriend he never told me about, so who knows what kind of other scandalous things he's been hiding from me. Maybe my parents even met for coffee, and now they're going to end up—

"Julie Dunham and I were friends," my mom says. "Best friends, really. We were like sisters. We did everything together, and then we—"

"Wait a minute." I hold up my hand to stop her. "How'd you know I was going to come here and ask you about Julie Dunham?" I slip my other hand into my bag and get ready to pull out my cell phone. If my dad thinks he can just call my mom behind my back and I'm going to be cool about it the way I was about his secret girlfriend, well, then he's got another thing coming. I'll call him right here, and the three of us will get this whole thing out on the table.

"Because," my mom says, looking surprised, "I can see ghosts too."

Chapter 2

"You can?" I ask. My hand loosens from around my cell phone, but I barely notice. My chest tightens with tension, but at the same time a weird sense of relief is flowing through me.

Because here's the thing: there's a part of me that has always thought that the fact that I can see ghosts might mean I'm kind of insane. That maybe there's something really wrong with me. Like, wrong in the you-might-need-to-be-locked-up-in-a-padded-room kind of way. "For how long?" I ask.

"As long as I can remember." She twists her hands in her lap. "From what I can tell, it's hereditary."

"It's hereditary?" I repeat dumbly.

She nods. "So I knew that Julie Dunham had been coming to see you, because she's been coming to see me, too." She licks her lips and swallows. "Do you want some cookies or something? I think I have some Oreos in the—"

"Wait! She's been coming to see you?" I ask.

My mom nods. "She's been telling me to talk to you, that I need to get you to stay away from Brandon."

"But *why* does she want me to stay away Brandon?" I demand.

"Because of me." My mom takes a deep breath. "Julie's very angry with me. She has been for years."

"Well, that's your problem," I say. "What do I have to do with it?" God, this tea is bitter. I reach for the sugar bowl and start spooning some in. I must be pretty angry, because granules spill out all over the table.

"Are you sure you want that much sugar?" my mom asks. "It's not good for you."

I look her in the eye and then dump another huge heaping spoonful right into my cup. If she thinks she has any right to play the parental card now, then she's definitely mistaken.

"O-kaayy," she says.

"Julie Dunham," I say. "Tell me. Now."

"Well, like I said, we were very close, like sisters." My mom turns and looks out the window, which faces her backyard. There are leaves falling from the trees, and if I weren't in such a bad mood, I'd think it was pretty. "And then I got pregnant with you, and Julie got pregnant with Brandon. My pregnancy was great, very smooth. But Julie . . . she had a hard time."

"What kind of a hard time?" I ask.

"Complications," my mom says. "High blood pressure, that kind of thing. Brandon came early, and when he did, she almost lost him."

"Oh my God," I say. "That's awful." And it is. I can't imagine how horrible and scary that must have been for her. But Brandon lived. And he's thirteen. So Julie might have to get over the whole overprotective thing. "But what does that have to do with you?"

"The night Julie had to go to the hospital, she called me." My mom's gaze is unfocused now. She's still staring out into her backyard, but she's not really looking at anything. "She wanted me to come and be with her. She was scared, and Brandon's dad was out of town at a conference. He was on his way home, but he had to take a flight, and he was stuck in Minneapolis because of a snowstorm."

She swallows, and I can tell how difficult it is for her to talk about this. I almost—*almost*—feel sorry for her. But not quite.

"So you weren't there for her?"

She shakes her head. "I was in the middle of helping a ghost move on, and it was something that couldn't wait. If

I didn't help the ghost then, she was going to be stuck here for God knows how long." Her eyes are filling with tears, and I hand her a napkin, realizing again how little I really know about my mom. Does she cry easily, or is this totally out of character for her?

"I thought I could get to the hospital in time, but it took longer than I thought, and by the time I got there, she'd lost a lot of blood. She was fine, but she'd been all alone. She never forgave me."

"So you guys just stopped being friends?"

My mom shakes her head. "Not right away. I tried to explain it to her. I told her about the ghosts. It was the first time I told anyone. Needless to say, she didn't believe me. And after a few weeks she stopped returning my calls."

I snort. "Sounds familiar."

She looks at me. "What do you mean?"

I shrug. "I told Brandon about seeing ghosts, and he didn't believe me. He basically accused me of being completely psychotic."

"Oh, Kendall," my mom says, sighing. I'm not sure if she's sighing because she thinks it's sad, or because she thinks I'm stupid for telling him. And honestly, I kind of don't care.

"Whatever," I say, deciding it's time to get back to the topic at hand. "Basically what you're telling me is that now that Julie Dunham is dead, she knows you were telling the truth about the ghosts?"

My mom nods.

"But then why is she so upset about me being with Brandon? Shouldn't she realize now that you weren't just making excuses? Shouldn't she want me and Brandon to be together forever to make up for her totally overreacting and not believing you?"

My mom looks up sharply from her tea. "You don't really think you're going to be with Brandon Dunham forever, do you?"

I'm about to ask her what's so wrong with Brandon Dunham when I realize she's just doing the normal mom thing and being all worried that I'm going to get carried away about a boy when I'm only in seventh grade.

All her parental concern is annoying. She doesn't have a *right* to be worried about me. If I'm going to get ridiculously attached to some boy, it's my own choice. My own decision. And she lost her right to say anything about those decisions when she left twelve years ago.

"I don't know," I say, just to be smart. I sit back in my chair and cross my arms over my chest. "Maybe I will marry him."

She gives me a sad smile, like she knows what I'm doing. Then she shakes her head. "Kendall," she says, "Julie Dunham isn't going to stop bothering you unless you and Brandon break up."

"But *why*?" I ask again.

"Because she knows the ghosts will always come first."

I frown. "What do you mean?"

"I mean that she knows Brandon will never be the first priority in your life. So she doesn't want the two of you to be together."

"Of course Brandon is going to be the first priority in my life," I say. I look around for Julie, almost hoping she's lurking in some corner somewhere so that she can hear this declaration. But she's nowhere to be found. The one time I actually want her here, she doesn't show up.

Whatever. She probably wouldn't believe me anyway. I mean, basically everything I've done these past few weeks has proven that I don't put Brandon before the ghosts.

But still. That doesn't mean I'm never going to. And Julie could have at least told me that was why she was getting so worked up. We could have talked about it. Like two rational adults.

"No." My mom shakes her head. "Kendall, she knows he's not the first priority. And that he never will be."

"How?"

"Because of what I did to her."

"Oh." It all clicks into place. Mrs. Dunham knows my mom wasn't there for her because of the ghosts, and now she's trying to protect Brandon from being with me so that he doesn't get hurt when I chose some ghost over him. But why should Mrs. Dunham judge me on the things my *mom* has done? And why does everyone have to be so up in my business? Seriously, it's like, focus on yourself.

"So what am I supposed to do?" I'm dangerously close to whining.

My mom shakes her head. "I can't answer that for you, Kendall."

"You *can't* answer that for me? Or *won't*?"

She shakes her head. "You need to figure this out yourself."

Okay, now I'm completely infuriated. I mean, think about it. First my mom takes off when I'm a baby. Then, when I show up at her house twelve years later looking for a little help, she won't give me any. Not to mention the fact that she obviously knew there was at least a *chance* I was going to be able to see ghosts and she left anyway! She never thought, oh, I don't know, *Maybe Kendall's going to be a little bit freaked out about this whole seeing-dead-people thing, so maybe I should think about someone other than myself for once and stick around so I can explain it to her.*

Talk about being selfish.

If she'd just done the right thing and stayed with me, I wouldn't be in this situation. If I'd known what was going on, I might have been able to calm Mrs. Dunham's fears before it got to this point. At the very least, my mom could have saved me from thinking I'm a complete and total crazy person every time a ghost showed up.

The anger that has been simmering my whole life, just waiting for someone to turn up the heat, boils up inside me.

I open my mouth to give my mom a piece of my mind, but then I realize I don't have the energy for some big scene. And then I start to wonder why I'm even here in the first place. My mom *left* me. When I was a *baby*. How can I expect a person who would do something like that to be any help whatsoever?

So after another moment of silence, I get up from the table and walk outside.

I halfway hope/expect my mom to stop me, but she doesn't.

The cab is sitting at the curb, right where I left it.

I climb inside.

"How'd it go?" the cabbie asks.

"No comment."

He nods, like he's used to driving people places where things don't go exactly as planned. "Back to the bus station?"

"Yes, please."

I fall asleep on the bus ride home. When I wake up, there's a crick in my neck, and my skin is all indented where my arm was pressing against the seat. Also, I'm pretty sure I was snoring.

The only thing that could make this ride worse would be if I missed my stop. Which, thankfully, I don't. (No thanks to the bus driver, who has, like, the softest voice ever. I really think bus drivers should be required to have loud, screaming voices. Otherwise, how are people going to wake up from their naps when it's time for them to get off?)

When I get outside the station, I find my bike in the bike rack, right where I left it a few hours ago. The cold air bites my cheeks, and I rub my hands together, then reach into my pocket and slip on my gloves.

I'm not looking forward to the ride home. It's going to be cold and long, and I'm sure that when I get there, my dad is going to ask me a million questions about where I've been and what I've been up to. And what am I going to say? There's no way I can tell him I went to see my mom. I left him a note this morning saying I was going to Ellie's, so hopefully he'll believe I was with her the whole time.

I'm so sick of all the lying that I don't know what to do with myself.

I ride home slowly, taking my time as I wind through the streets. I know the faster I ride, the warmer I'll get and the quicker I'll get home and out of the cold, but my legs have no energy. I should be refreshed from the nap I took on the bus, but I'm not. I'm lethargic and woozy. It's like my emotional energy is so low, it's starting to interfere with my physical energy.

When I finally get to my house, there's a note in the kitchen right next to the one I left my dad this morning. He's out doing some furniture shopping with his girlfriend, Cindy, at the outlets.

So while I was worried about *him* worrying about *me*, he was out having fun with Cindy. They were probably picking out furniture for some new house they're planning on moving into without me. Maybe even a crib for a dumb baby they're going to end up having, and it won't see ghosts because it won't have my mom's screwed-up genes, and they'll love it so much that they'll totally forget about me.

I'm being dramatic and going into a complete shame spiral, and I don't even care.

All I want to do right now is feel sorry for myself.

So I decide to really wallow.

First I run upstairs and change into my favorite pajamas—pink-and-maroon-plaid pants and a matching shirt. Then I slide on a pair of soft and cozy lime-green socks. I pull my hair back into a simple ponytail, because honestly, what's the point of doing my hair? It's not like I have anyone to see or anywhere to go.

When I'm all dressed, I head back downstairs and pour myself a big glass of milk, then pull a package of cookie dough out of the refrigerator. I know it's totally cliché to be gorging myself on disgusting food, but I don't care. I plop the whole roll of dough into a bowl and then bring it upstairs, where I turn on my computer and start streaming a cheesy romantic comedy.

I watch and eat, the whole time realizing how completely unrealistic the movie is. I mean, really, who thinks it's a good idea to send these kinds of messages to young girls? That some guy who's super-good-looking and popular is going to fall in love with them even though they're "normal"? It's all a big joke of a lie.

Still. These Hollywood types might be onto something, because I'm kind of into this movie. The popular guy is really hot. He looks like a young Channing Tatum. And he's not even that much of a jerk. He's just, you know, *misunderstood.*

Soon I'm at the part of the movie where the "nerdy" girl is about to get a makeover from her friends, causing the hero to realize the girl was beautiful this whole time, she just needed to take her glasses off and learn how to use some eye shadow.

I kind of hate myself for liking this movie, if you want to know the truth. How can taking your glasses off make you beautiful? Glasses are super-cute and trendy. I've even thought about getting some of those fake Kate Spade ones. Although they're really expensive, and I'd probably break them because I'm always—

DING-DONG.

The sound of the doorbell ringing causes me to drop

my cookie dough spoon. I look down at the almost-empty bowl. Wow. I didn't realize how much I'd eaten. The label says it has sixteen servings. Yikes.

The doorbell rings again. Probably a door-to-door salesman. Solicitors aren't supposed to be allowed in this town, but sometimes they don't listen. Like this one cable company that's always coming around, trying to get people to switch their service. My dad has called the police on them, like, five times, but no one ever does anything.

I turn the volume on the computer up a couple of notches to drown out the doorbell. A blob of cookie dough falls onto the keyboard. I pick it up and pop it into my mouth. It's official—I've hit a completely new level of disgustingness.

After another minute the doorbell rings again, followed by the sound of someone pounding on the door.

I glance out the window to see if I can spot a truck with the name of a company on it. I'm in just the right mood to call the town and lodge a complaint.

But there's no truck in the driveway.

I crane my neck so I can look down the street and see if there's a truck parked down the block. Sometimes these scoundrels try to get creative and hide their vehicle so people think they're Girl Scouts or something.

There's no truck down the block.

But there *is* a purple bike parked in my side yard.

A purple bike I would know anywhere.

A purple bike that belongs to my best friend, Ellie.

My hearts leaps into my throat.

Ellie's here!

Ellie rode her bike all the way over here, which only means one thing. She wants to make up!

Oh. Right. In addition to all my other problems, I forgot to mention that Ellie and I are in a fight. See, I was helping this ghost named Lyra, and I needed to get close to her brother, Micah. But obviously I couldn't tell Ellie the reason I needed to spend time with Micah. So when she caught me hanging out with him at the bowling alley, she was mad because I'd lied to her about where I was. Also she thought I must have a crush on Micah, which is totes ridiculous because hello, I like Brandon.

I throw a sweatshirt on over my pajama top and fly down the stairs.

She's still pounding on the door. Wow. She must really want to make up.

I fling it open mid-pound.

Ellie stares at me.

"Hi!" I say brightly.

She looks me up and down. "You're in your pajamas."

"Yeah." I shake out my ponytail and smooth my hair back. "I was watching a movie."

She blinks. "It's only four o'clock."

"I wanted to be comfy. You want to come in? I have extra pajamas and socks. We could watch movies together. I'm eating cookie dough."

"I know," she says. "You have some on your cheek."

"Oh." I reach up and brush it off. It falls onto the porch with a plop.

Then I notice there's a big cardboard box sitting behind Ellie on the porch. She picks it up and holds it out to me.

"Here."

I take it. Wow. This thing is heavy. "Wow," I say, "this is heavy. You rode this over here all by yourself?"

"Yup."

"Okay." I'm having trouble seeing her over the top of the box. "Do you want to come in and open it with me?"

"*Open* it with you?" she asks, sounding kind of aghast.

"Yeah. It's a present, right?" What else would it be? Although I'm kind of embarrassed that she brought me a make-up gift. I didn't get her anything, and I'm the one who should be apologizing. Maybe I can bring her shopping so she can pick out her own present. Or maybe I'll make her a scrapbook or something.

Ooh, or one of those coupon books that you can trade in for, like, an hour of BFF time or something. I used to think those were kind of lame, but if I make the coupons worth something really good, it could definitely work.

"No, it's not a present," Ellie says. Then she reaches out

and yanks the box right out of my hands and drops it onto the porch. Wow. It sounds like something might have broken in there.

"Then what is it?" I ask.

But I get my answer soon enough, because Ellie's down on her knees now, pulling things out of the box. My red sweater. A picture of us together at the beach. An orange sundress we each bought so we could dress like twins. A copy of an essay we wrote about bullying that got published in the school newspaper. My old iPod that I left at her house, the one that has this awesome playlist on it that we use to have crazy dance parties.

And then I get it. This isn't a make-up box at all. It's a BFF *breakup* box.

"It's all here," Ellie's saying as she pulls more things out of the box and drops them onto the porch. One sleeve of my red sweater dangles over the edge of the porch and falls into a mud puddle. Ew.

"Um," I say. "Okay. But, um, don't you think we should talk about this?"

"Here's your purse that you left at my house after the sixth-grade dance, and I have your watch somewhere, but I couldn't find it, so I can give it to you when I see you at school." She stands up and brushes her jeans off and then looks at me. "Or maybe I'll just mail it to you."

I don't say anything, mostly because I don't know

what to say. I've never seen Ellie so angry before. It doesn't make sense. She's usually so levelheaded and calm. And now she has shown up at my house like some kind of crazy person and has begun throwing my stuff all over the porch.

"Well?" she demands. "Aren't you going to give me my stuff back?"

"Your stuff?"

"Yeah." She pulls a piece of folded paper out of her jeans pocket. "You have my fuzzy gray slippers, my dangling heart earrings, and my curling iron, plus that book I lent you, the one about the girl who lives in Victorian England and falls in love with the servant boy."

"Oh. Right. That book was really good."

"I know," she says. "I'm the one who told you to read it."

"Yeah." I swallow hard. It's just starting to hit me now how upset she is. I never would have imagined Ellie acting like this. It's like she's a different person.

"Listen, Ellie," I say, "can't we talk about this? I mean, this is pretty drastic, don't you think?"

"Is it?" she asks. *"Is it?"*

"Well, kind of," I say. I sidestep the dress that's on the front porch and sit down. I'm hoping she's going to sit down next to me, but she doesn't. She just stands there.

I pull my sweatshirt tighter around me. The sky has turned completely gray, and the air is cold against my skin.

"Unfortunately, the drastic-ness of this situation is not really for you to decide," Ellie says.

"You didn't seem that mad when I saw you at the Y earlier," I point out.

"I'm allowed to change my feelings," she says defensively. "Besides, the more I thought about it, the more I realized how upset I was. It was not cool to lie to me, Kendall Williams. Not cool at all."

"I know." I look down at my hands, shame and horror bubbling up inside me. I don't know what to do. I want to tell Ellie why I lied to her about being with Micah, but I can't. I can't risk her having the same reaction as Brandon. I've probably lost him forever, and I don't know what I would do if I lost Ellie forever too.

I start to cry, the warm tears making tracks down my face. One of them hits my lip, and I lick it away, tasting the sad saltiness.

My crying must soften something in Ellie, because she sits down next to me. Her body language is still pretty obvious, though—her legs are tilted away from me and her arms are crossed, her knees pulled up close to her body.

"Why did you do it?" Ellie asks. "I wouldn't have been upset if you'd told me you liked Micah. I wouldn't have cared. You're my best friend. We're supposed to talk about everything."

"I don't like Micah," I say.

She stands up and starts to walk away, like she doesn't believe me and she's done with this conversation.

"Ellie," I say, and she stops. "I swear, I don't like Micah."

She turns back around toward me. "Then why did you bother lying about being with him? When you could have been with me and Brandon and Kyle?"

I take a deep breath. This is the moment I should tell her the truth, about me and the ghosts, and just hope that somehow, some way, she believes me. I mean, if I lie to her now, eventually I'm going to have to lie to her again—there will always be some other ghost, some other situation. And at some point my lies are going to catch up with me. Look what happened with my mom and Julie Dunham.

So I should definitely tell Ellie the truth.

Right now.

"I just . . . I felt bad for him," I lie.

"You felt *bad* for him?" she repeats incredulously.

"Yeah. I didn't want him to not have any friends—you know, because he's new—so I decided to hang out with him." This excuse makes no sense, and the words sound strangled and hollow, even to me. Ellie knows me better than anyone else in the world, and so there's no way she's going to believe me.

Sure enough, she says, "You wanted Micah to have friends so bad that you were willing to lie to your *best* friend and your *boy*friend about hanging out with him?"

"Yes. Um, because I knew Brandon wouldn't really want me hanging out with him. Even as friends. And I knew you'd probably be mad about it too."

"You didn't even give us a chance!" Ellie yells. "You didn't even try to explain to us what was going on. You just lied and snuck around behind our backs."

"I know," I say, glancing down at my hands in shame. "I'm sorry."

Ellie shakes her head. She stands there for a minute, just looking at me. She has an expression on her face that I've never seen before. It's a mixture of sadness and disappointment, and it makes me feel like my heart is breaking in two. I can tell that even though she doesn't believe me, she *wants* to believe me. She wants to go back to being friends. She wants to convince herself I'm telling the truth.

It's actually pretty horrible, when you think about it. That my best friend cares about me so much that even when it's obvious I'm lying, she's still struggling with it because she wants so badly to believe me.

But the absolute *worst* part about the whole situation is that I *want* Ellie to believe me. I want her to believe my lie. Because I'm too much of a coward to tell her the truth and risk losing her friendship.

She takes a step back toward me, and for a second I think she's going to sit down again. But then she shakes her head.

"I'm sorry, Kendall," she says, her face hardening. "But I don't believe you."

And then she turns around and walks away before getting back on her bike and pedaling down my driveway.

I sit there in the cold for a few minutes, hoping maybe she's going to change her mind and come back. But of course she doesn't. And so when my hands go numb and my nose gets cold, I finally get up, pick up all the stuff Ellie brought over, and head back into the house.

Chapter 3

If you were to guess that the rest of my weekend is a complete nightmare, you'd be totally right.

All I want to do is hide out in my room, but instead I end up having to help my dad and Cindy arrange their new furniture. You'd think they'd be able to handle it themselves, but apparently not. Apparently they need the help of a twelve-year-old who's not even that strong.

(They really did need all the help they could get, though. They were trying to move a love seat, a chair, and a sofa all by themselves. It was pretty ridiculous, especially since they had to make three trips back to the store to pick everything up. My dad kept saying, "Paying two hundred dollars for delivery is a waste of money when you can just do it yourself!"

Which I guess is true, but when you accidentally dent the wall in two spots and you're going to have to spend time fixing it, I'm not sure it's that much of a bargain. Plus I'm pretty sure Cindy hurt her shoulder when we moved that last chair. She tried to pretend it wasn't a big deal, but I caught her wincing a few times when she thought no one was looking.)

Anyway, when I'm not playing mover, I spend the rest of the weekend doing my homework and hanging out in my room.

The only upside to the weekend is that, as bad as it is, it's still better than going to school. I mean, how awful is that going to be? Seeing Brandon and Ellie and Kyle, all having fun and being together without me? Shudder.

When my alarm goes off on Monday, I resist the urge to reach out and throw my clock across the room. I snuggle under the covers and wonder if I can fake being sick. It's not completely out of the realm of possibility. Yesterday my dad kept asking me if everything was okay, since I spent so much time in my room. I told him everything was fine, but now that I think about it, maybe I was coming down with something.

I reach for my phone and start to google "diseases that can come on within twenty-four hours and require you to stay home from school" when there's a knock on my bedroom door.

I quickly shove my phone under the covers and shut my eyes.

"Kendall?" my dad asks softly.

I pretend to be sleeping. Obviously, a sick person wouldn't wake up right away.

"Kendall?" he asks, a little louder. I hear the soft creak of the door opening. "Kendall!" my dad says, this time a lot more urgently.

The kind of urgency that would probably wake up someone who was ill. I open my eyes and blink in what I hope is a sick-seeming way.

"Oh," I say, trying to look startled and confused, like I'm so out of it, I forgot the world actually existed. "Hi," I croak.

"I'm leaving for work," he says. "I have an early job."

"Okay." I sit up and put my hand to my head. "Does it feel hot in here to you?"

"No."

"It feels hot in here to me." It really would have been better to come up with this plan last night. Then I could have maybe put a warm washcloth on my face so I could look all warm and flushed and feverish. Now I'm going to have to depend on my acting skills, which aren't stellar, especially under pressure.

"I'm leaving," my dad repeats. I'm just about to tell him I'm not feeling well when he says, "And don't even bother to pretend being sick. You're going to school."

And then he closes my bedroom door without saying anything else.

I sigh and lie back down on my pillow. How did he know I wasn't really sick? Am I that transparent? And what if I really was sick? Then he'd be sorry, sending me off to school when I could be on my deathbed.

Whatever.

It's just school. I've been going to school every day since I was five. And back then I didn't know a single soul. Of course, my day was pretty awful. I ended up standing by the coat closet for, like, five minutes at recess, because I was too afraid to go outside without any friends.

But still. It's not like I don't have *any* other friends at school. There's that girl in my homeroom, Kayla Pies, who has always been really nice to me. And there's another girl in my math class who sits with us at lunch sometimes, Deanna Meacham.

With all my scheming about being sick, I have to get up immediately or I'm going to miss the bus. So I jump into the shower, then quickly arrange my hair into a twisty braid that starts near my forehead and goes all the way down the side of my head. It's super-easy to do, but it's super-cute, and will look even cuter when it dries.

The sun is peeking through the clouds, but it's low in the sky, and I can tell it's chilly out. So I pick out my comfiest pair of jeans and a soft pink sweater, hoping that the softness of the denim and the presence of my favorite color will calm me.

I top the outfit off with cozy pink socks, my cream-colored UGG boots that I had to do hours and hours of chores to convince my dad to buy for me, and my puffy black jacket.

I pack my book bag, grab a few dollars out of the jar on top of the fireplace for lunch money, and head to the bus stop.

As soon as I get to school, there they are.

The three of them.

Ellie.

Brandon.

Kyle.

All standing in the lobby by the front entrance.

Ellie's cheeks are red from the cold, and she's laughing at something Kyle's saying. She throws her head back, her hair falling away from her face, and then Brandon adds something, and the three of them all laugh together.

My throat gets tight, and tears prickle at the back of my eyes. I stay frozen in place, unable to move. It's like the three of them are a movie or something and I can't stop watching.

A second later Brandon catches me looking. I avert my gaze and start to walk by, catching glimpses of him out of the corner of my eye as I weave between kids that are all hurrying to their lockers before homeroom. He's not laughing anymore, and I expect him to look away.

But he doesn't, and so finally I turn and look back at him.

We stay like that, just looking at each other, and it's like everyone else fades away. My heart has stopped in my chest. It literally feels like I can't breathe. And for a split second I convince myself I can fix things.

I'll go over there, and I'll tell him I need to talk to him and Ellie, and then I'll explain everything to them, and maybe they'll believe me. Maybe if I can just tell them something that makes more sense, if I can prove to Brandon that—

But then he looks away.

And the first bell rings.

Ellie and Kyle hurry down the hall.

Brandon heads the other way, down toward the science wing where his homeroom is.

And there's nothing left for me to do but go to class.

Math.

Brandon Dunham is sitting right in front of me.

I used to think that I was so lucky. That I could just be in math, sitting behind Brandon Dunham, being able to stare at his neck the whole time. (Brandon Dunham has a very cute neck, in case you were wondering.)

But today it seems like some kind of cruel joke. What a

mistake, dating someone from my own school. Think about it—why would I want to date someone I have to see every single day? Of *course* we were going to break up eventually. And now look what I have to deal with—the back of Brandon Dunham's neck. Every. Single. Day.

Jessa Schneider has the right idea. She's this girl in my social studies class who's always dating boys from other schools. Of course, everyone pretty much knows she's lying about it. She has all these cell phone pics she's always waving around of all the guys she's supposedly dating. There's, like, a new one every week, and they're all super-cute. How many super-cute guys from other schools can she really be meeting?

Not to mention that they always have these super-amazing stories to go along with their great looks. They're always, like, captain of the football team, or head of the student council.

Jessa's probably stealing those photos from random people's Facebook pages. That might be illegal. I wonder if someone—

"Kendall Williams," Mr. Jacobi says.

"Here," I say automatically.

Everyone in the class laughs.

"I wasn't asking if you were *here*," Mr. Jacobi says. "I was reminding you about the math tutoring project at Stoneridge Elementary. It starts today."

"Oh. Right. Totally." I give him a smile, even though I completely forgot about that dumb project. It's this after-school program where we're supposed to spend time with elementary school kids who need help with their math.

I signed up for it during the first week of school, and the only reason I did was because Brandon signed up. This was before I knew him and was just staring at his neck. I thought maybe we'd get to know each other if we were involved in the same activities.

"So the people whose names I just called will stay after school today," Mr. Jacobi says, "and we will head over to Stoneridge. Once you're there, you will be paired up with a student who needs your help. The work is elementary school level, so I'm sure you'll have no trouble handling it."

I'm not sure if it's my imagination or not, but I feel like maybe he looks at me a little doubtfully when he says that last part. Like I'm the only one he's worried about being able to teach little kids. Which is super-insulting when you think about it. I mean, yeah, math's not my best subject, but I can totally help kindergartners. They're probably just learning how to count. They probably don't even need tutors.

In fact, this whole thing seems like something schools do to make it look like they're getting involved in community service. It's all very political.

"You'll be assigned peer partners in class to help you," Mr. Jacobi says. "That way, if you encounter any problems, you'll be able to get together with your peers and brainstorm teaching solutions."

Yawn.

Someone in the back raises their hand. "Will we be able to get class time to do this?"

"Yes," Mr. Jacobi says. Then he narrows his eyes and pushes his glasses up on his nose. "But let me remind you that this is to be taken seriously. This is *not* an easy way to get extra credit. These children are your students. They are going to be depending on you to teach them and be good role models. You're going to need to work hard to come up with a lesson plan that's going to be successful, just like a real teacher."

Again his eyes flick over to me. Really, what is this guy's problem? I'm getting a lot better in math. And I'm really trying. And now that Brandon isn't going to be a distraction, I'll probably get even better.

Of course, Brandon was helping me with my math, but whatever. I don't need him. I can do great on my own. I sit up straighter, determined to pay attention. I open my notebook to a blank page, making it my new resolution to take perfect notes on everything Mr. Jacobi says.

"Be a role model to kids," I write, and then draw a little

flower next to it. Who wants to read their notes back if they're not fancy? Probably if people kept their notes nice and doodley, they'd be a lot better off. In school and in life.

"Now, I've put you in groups of three," Mr. Jacobi says.

"Working in groups of three," I write, with a little smiley face after it. Wow. I am a really good note taker. I mean, I'm not missing a thing.

"I'll read the partners now."

I'm writing *"Mr. Jacobi will read the partners"* and realizing that might be taking it a little too far when Mr. Jacobi calls my name.

"Kendall, Brandon, and Madison," he says. "You three will be working together. When you arrive at the elementary school this afternoon, we will have a short informational meeting, and then you will be assigned the names of your students. Now please take out your weekend homework so we can go over it. I'm sure you're all struggling with something."

My blood is rushing through my body so fast, I can hear it. My face feels flushed and hot. Me, Brandon, and Madison are going to be working together? It's bad enough I'm going to have to be with Brandon, but *Madison Baker*? Madison Baker is this seriously annoying girl who has a big crush on Brandon. She's actually part of the reason

Brandon got so upset about me hanging out with Micah. Madison kept telling Brandon that I was spending a lot of time at Micah's mom's nail salon, hanging out with Micah. Which was true, but still. She didn't have to go blabbing it all over the place.

I sneak a glance over my shoulder to where Madison's sitting a few rows away. She smirks at me and then waves her fingers. She's wearing a tight white skirt and a long-sleeved red top. Her hair falls in silky waves over her shoulders, and her lip gloss is perfectly applied. As she waves, a shiny Michael Kors watch slides delicately down her wrist.

I swallow and turn around, forcing myself to pay attention.

It's okay, I tell myself. I'll just tell Mr. Jacobi that I can't do this whole tutoring program thing. I'll tell him I have other, more personal commitments that have come up. I'm sure it happens all the time.

When the bell rings, I take my time gathering my books so that I can stay and talk to Mr. Jacobi after everyone else leaves.

"Hey." Madison Baker appears in front of me. She leans down, resting her hand on my desk for support, but you can tell she's just doing it so she can show off her watch. She wants to make me jealous. And it kind of works. I mean, it's a really fab watch. And I'm only human.

"Oh, hi," I say nonchalantly. I open my folder and start flipping through the papers, pretending I'm looking for something important.

"So, looks like we're going to be working together," she says, giving me a big smile.

"Yeah, looks like it."

"Should be fun," she says.

She's so fake, I can't stand it. She knows it's not going to be fun. How could it be fun? She doesn't like me, and I don't like her. And I'm sure neither of us likes tutoring.

"Yeah, totally," I say, mostly because I just want her to go away. I'm not about to tell her we're not going to be working together because I'm going to be quitting the project. It's not worth getting into.

"I'm really sorry about you and Brandon breaking up." She reaches her hand out and squeezes my shoulder.

"How did you know we broke up?" I ask before I can stop myself. I'm not sure I want to know the answer. What if Brandon called her immediately after we broke up and was all, *Oh, hi, Madison. I'm single now. Wanna hang out?* I'm so not in a place to handle that kind of information.

Madison shrugs. "I didn't see you guys together this morning, so I just figured." She sounds gleeful, like she's glad she guessed right. "How are you doing?"

"I'm fine," I say, struggling to keep my voice even.

"Yeah, but you must be at least a little sad," she says. She's studying my face, trying to make sure I'm miserable. "I mean, he broke up with you."

I keep rearranging the papers in my folder, making sure I don't make eye contact with her. If I have to see her standing there with her dumb watch and her dumb hair and her dumb perfect makeup, I'm going to either scream or cry. And neither one of those things would be good, especially since Mr. Jacobi is still at his desk. I don't think he can hear what we're saying, but he's looking at us impatiently, like he can't wait for us to leave so he can do whatever it is teachers do when their students aren't around.

I don't say anything for a beat, hoping maybe Madison will just go away.

But of course she doesn't.

"Poor Kendall," she coos, and gives my hair a quick stroke. "If you need someone to talk to, I'm totally here for you." She tilts her head and thinks about it. "Not that anyone has ever broken up with *me* before. But I'm a really good listener when my friends are going through it."

This statement is wrong on so many levels. First of all, she's totally snobby for pointing out that no one has ever broken up with her. It's probably true, but still. How ridiculous.

And second, Madison Baker and I are not friends. We never have been, and we never will be. So for her to even suggest that I would talk to her about what's going on with me and Brandon is preposterous. Obviously, she just wants to get gossip out of me. The only person I would talk about this with is Ellie, even though I can't, since she's pretty much not speaking to me.

I feel a warm tide of anger moving through me, starting in my toes and filling my body until it builds to a crash. A crash that must turn me into a complete and total lunatic, because before I know it, I'm saying something I shouldn't be saying. Something that isn't even true. Something that could cause more harm than good.

"Well," I say, flicking my folder shut with a satisfied slap. "I *should* be sad, yeah. But I'm not. I mean, the reason Brandon broke up with me was because he was jealous of me and Micah. You know, Micah from the hair salon?" I flip my hair over my shoulder on this last part, mostly because it seems like something you would do when you're delivering a particularly bratty line. "I started to really like him, and of course, I was trying to juggle both of them at the same time, but Brandon found out." I roll my eyes. "So in a way, *I* kind of broke up with *him*."

Madison's face darkens, her eyes narrowing into two tiny slits. "You like Micah?" she asks skeptically.

"Well, yeah," I say. "Didn't you know that already? I mean, you were always telling Brandon how much time I was spending at the salon with him."

She has the decency to look a little guilty. "Well, yeah," she says. "You *were* always there."

"Yeah," I say. "Because I liked him. I mean, uh, *like* him. Present tense. Anyway, when we started hanging out and everything, you know, Brandon got upset. And he caught me at the bowling alley with Micah, and so he broke up with me."

I'm surprised at how easily this slips out of my mouth. Of course, only part of it is a lie. Brandon *did* catch me at the bowling alley with Micah, I *had* lied about it, and Brandon *did* break up with me. But I don't like Micah, at least not as more than a friend. And of course I leave out the part about telling Brandon I can see ghosts.

"Oh," Madison says. "Well, that's good. So you're with Micah now?"

I roll my eyes. "I don't really want a boyfriend right now," I say. "That's how I got into this mess in the first place." The idea that I would be in so much trouble because I had a boyfriend and would now want the chance to play the field is almost laughable. I'm so not that type. In fact, before I got together with Brandon, my experience with boys was pretty much zero.

And Madison must know it, because she wrinkles up her nose and gives me a look. "I guess," she says. Then she leans in so close that I can smell her perfume and see the perfect smooth line of her eyeliner. "But if I were you, I'd be careful. You don't want to give up any opportunities with guys when you have them. You never know when they're going to be gone."

And then she pats me on the head.

Madison Baker actually pats me on the head!

Talk about condescending.

"Anyway," she says in this totally bored tone, like I've been making her stand here talking about my boring boy problems, when she's the one who started this stupid conversation in the first place. Then she reaches down into my book bag and pulls out my cell phone.

"Cute phone," she says as she begins to program her number into it. "Here's my number. Text me anytime. You know, if you need to talk. Or if you need any advice about how to act around Micah."

She slides my phone back into my bag. I don't say anything, mostly because I'm kind of stunned. I mean, who does that? Just reaches into someone's bag and pulls out their phone? Talk about a total breach of etiquette and privacy. What if I had something really embarrassing on there?

"Bye!" she says, like we've been having a totally pleasant conversation and we're not mortal enemies and she didn't try to just ruin my life and my relationship.

I sigh and pull out my phone, studying it for signs of vandalism. I think about erasing her number, but something inside me decides not to. I'm not sure why—it's not like I'm ever going to call her.

But deleting it would mean that I care. And I don't. Madison Baker is nothing to me. She's just a little fly that's buzzing around my head, totally inconsequential to me and my life. Well. If a fly had a crush on my ex-boyfriend and had beautiful hair and flawless makeup.

The thought of a fly wearing makeup is ridiculous. I laugh out loud. I mean, can you imagine? Like, a fly with painted wings? Although, when you think about it, it's not really any different than us painting our nails or dyeing our hair. Humans are just animals, after all. And in other cultures—

"Something funny, Miss Williams?" Mr. Jacobi asks.

Oh. Right. I'm still in math.

And Mr. Jacobi is still sitting at his desk.

And I'm still sitting at my desk, which is ridiculous, since the bell rang a few minutes ago and everyone else is already gone.

"Oh, um, no," I say, standing up quickly and gathering my books.

"Is there a reason you're still in my classroom?" Mr. Jacobi asks.

Wow. Talk about making a student feel unwelcome and unwanted. Someone really ought to file a complaint about him.

"Yes, actually," I say. I walk up to the front of the room. "I wanted to talk to you about the tutoring program."

"Don't worry, Miss Williams," he says. His head is completely down, and he's focused on the papers he's grading. He's not even looking at me. "It's elementary school math. You shouldn't have any problems with it."

I do my best not to feel insulted. "Oh, it's not that. I'm sure I'll have no problem with the math. It's just that, uh, I'm not going to be able to do the program."

This gets his attention. He sits up straight and takes off his glasses, regarding me across his desk. "And why is that, Miss Williams?"

"Well," I say slowly. "I have, um, a family situation going on."

"What kind of family situation?" he asks, sounding suspicious.

"It's personal." I'm hoping this will suffice, since obviously there is no family situation. I put what I hope is a serious look on my face and quickly rack my brain, trying to think of something I could use that wouldn't technically be a lie. I could tell him about my dad's high cholesterol. Although, that's not really a pressing situation, and besides, I don't want to tempt fate by exaggerating my dad's health problems. I mean, that would so not be cool.

Ooh, I could use the excuse of me getting a new stepmother. Of course, my dad and his girlfriend, Cindy, aren't engaged, but they are in a pretty serious relationship. My dad gave her a promise ring so that she wouldn't move to Virginia and everything. And besides, everyone knows teenagers have tons of problems when it comes to blended families. Especially me, since I obviously have abandonment issues due to my mother leaving me when I was young. Mr. Jacobi doesn't know about that, but I wouldn't mind telling him.

Still, it's always risky when you start talking about having a hard time at home, because teachers are usually quick to send you to the guidance counselor's office. Honestly, has anyone ever really been helped by the guidance counselors? Mine is named Ms. Westlake, and I see her once a year to get scheduled for my classes.

"That's fine, Miss Williams," Mr. Jacobi says.

"Really?" Wow. He's not even going to make me explain myself? Yay! Looks like my luck is turning around.

"Yes, really," he says.

"Thank you for understanding, Mr. Jacobi," I say seriously, and then start to head out of the classroom. I want to go running out into the hall in celebration, but I control myself. Someone dealing with a pressing personal issue would not be running in jubilation.

"Oh, Miss Williams?" Mr. Jacobi calls after me.

I turn around. "Yes?"

"I feel it's only fair to let you know that if you don't

get this extra credit, you will be in danger of failing my class."

"Failing?"

"Yes." He licks his finger and turns a page in his grade book, looking for my name. How gross, licking his finger like that. I make a mental note to wash my hands every time he hands a paper back to me. Who knows what kind of germs I've been exposed to.

"How is that possible?" I knew things were bad, but I had no idea I was in danger of failing the class.

"Well, the midterm counts for thirty percent of your grade."

"But we haven't had our midterm yet."

"Well, if you don't do this extra credit, you would need to get at least a B on the midterm to make sure you pull up the rest of your grade. And if you do not achieve at least a B on the midterm, you will fail the class. And then, Miss Williams, I will be seeing you again next year."

Oh. My. God. Next year? With Mr. Jacobi? There's no way I'm going to get less than a B on the midterm. I don't care if I have to study for, like, a month straight. Of course, I don't have Brandon to help me anymore. But still. Another whole year with Mr. Jacobi? I can't think of anything worse than that.

And do I really want to risk it? Just because I'm afraid of Madison Baker?

I sigh. "I'll be there this afternoon," I say.

"Great," Mr. Jacobi says, and then he gives me a satisfied smile. "I'm looking forward to it."

Ugh.

Chapter

4

Why is it that when you have something fun to do after school, like going shopping, the day seems to drag on forever? And when you have something you're dreading, the minutes seem like seconds and the hours seem like minutes? Before I know it, the day is over and it's time to gather in the lobby to head over to the elementary school.

Stoneridge Elementary is only a couple of blocks away from the middle school. It's a brand-new building that was built the year after I graduated from elementary school. Which is really unfair when you think about it. Also, why did they build a new elementary school? Everyone knows that little kids don't care about things like what their school looks like. They're just happy to actually be in school.

Anyway, whoever it is who's in charge of these things (the principal?) has apparently decided that in an effort to save money, we're going to be walking over to the elementary school instead of taking a bus.

This fact is making Mr. Jacobi very angry.

"Apparently, saving money is more important to some people than student safety," he grumbles as he does a head count. "And now it's up to me to make sure none of you get hit by a car."

He glares at the group of us, like he just knows someone is going to be stupid enough to get hit by a car. Not that I can blame him. I glance over at Jason Fields, who's running around the lobby with his hands outstretched, pretending to be an airplane circling in for a landing.

I can't believe they think it's okay for him to go and tutor elementary school students. I mean, look at him. He's obviously like an elementary school student himself. He's been doing that same move since second grade.

Mr. Jacobi checks us all off on a list, and then we move through the door and out into the fall day.

The air is colder than I expected, and I reach into my pockets to pull out my purple-and-lavender-striped gloves. My fingers instantly warm up, but a little shiver runs through my body anyway.

Wearing the gloves reminds me of a couple weeks

ago, when Brandon, Kyle, Ellie, and I all went ice-skating together. It was one of the first times that I felt like Brandon and I were a real couple.

But that was before. Before everything turned into a huge mess, before Brandon broke up with me, before the three of them started hating me.

I will not cry, I will not cry, I will not cry.

I force myself to look straight ahead and focus on the horizon in front of me. I read somewhere that you should do that if you're in a boat and you start to feel seasick. Something about how focusing on one spot is supposed to make you feel grounded. Maybe it'll work for feeling sick to your stomach about your best friend and your boyfriend both ditching you.

Surprisingly, my new focusing-on-the-horizon technique does make me start to feel better, but after a second or two I start to get distracted by the fact that I can see Brandon walking a few yards ahead of me. I let out a sigh of relief when I see he's not walking with Madison.

In fact, I don't see Madison anywhere. Is it possible that maybe she decided not to do this whole tutoring thing? Leave it to Madison Baker to figure out a way to get out of it. She probably sweet-talked Mr. Jacobi into letting her quit. And her math grades probably aren't any better than mine. I mean, I don't see how they can be. She never takes any notes.

I glance around, looking for Madison, and I finally spot her a few rows back. She's chattering away to someone I can't see. Probably one of her little minions, the puppy-dog-like girls who follow her around and make her feel important. Seriously, how can people not see through her?

I sigh and keep walking. I can see the elementary school in the distance now, and I forget about my plan to keep my eyes fixed on the horizon. Instead I keep them locked on the ground, just concentrating on putting one foot in front of the other.

If I have to be in a group with Brandon and Madison, I don't have to be obsessed with looking at them. In fact, I really shouldn't care about them at all. Brandon's not my boyfriend anymore. He's not even my friend. And so what he does is none of my business.

I am a secure, confident woman. And if Brandon isn't secure enough to handle the fact that I can see ghosts, well then, that's his problem, not mine.

Although.

One quick look at Brandon wouldn't hurt, would it? I mean, it's not like I'm obsessed with him or anything. And when you think about it, it's probably better to know where he is. You know, so that I can make sure to avoid him.

I peek back up toward the front of our class, but I can't see Brandon anymore. His perfectly highlighted (naturally, of course—Brandon would never do anything like highlight his hair—he's way too manly for that) head is nowhere to be seen.

I glance behind me, but I don't see Madison anywhere either. I'm about to kind of freak out when I spot her, walking with Allison Lee.

Hmm. Maybe this whole not-trying-to-keep-my-eyes-on-them thing isn't the best strategy. Maybe telling myself that I *shouldn't* be watching them is going to make me want to watch them even more. It's, like, too tempting.

I slow down my pace a little bit and move to the left of the crowd. I walk even more slowly until, finally, Madison is ahead of me. I'm so stealth! She didn't even notice that I was dropping behind her so that I could spy on her.

Of course, this is probably because she's totally self-involved. I mean, right now she's telling Allison Lee all about the new pool her dad's putting in just for her, and how he's making it aqua because that's her favorite color. Which is kind of ridiculous. I mean, aren't all pools aqua? I highly doubt her dad got an aqua pool just because she wanted it.

What if her favorite color was brown? Was her dad going to get an ugly brown pool? I doubt it. That would have been horrible for property values. And grown-ups are always worried about property values. At least that was the excuse my dad used when I wanted to paint ladybugs all over the outside of our house in the third grade. I was really mad at him at the time, but now I'm grateful. Could you imagine being in seventh grade and living in a ladybug house? How humiliating.

I'm at the back of the pack now, and I quicken my step just a little bit so that I don't fall too far behind. Now that I'm not walking as fast, I'm starting to get cold, and I take my hat out of my pocket and pull it down over my ears.

"Cute hat," a girl's voice says behind me.

"Thank you," I say automatically. I turn around to see who it is behind me, especially since I thought I was the last one in line.

It's an older girl, maybe around eighteen or nineteen, with curly brown hair and full lips. Her cheeks are flushed, but in an adorable way, not in a wow-it's-cold-out-and-I-look-a-mess kind of way.

"Are you a volunteer?" I ask. A lot of times when we have field trips, they bring along some high school or college volunteers to make sure none of us get into trouble.

She frowns. "I'm Madison's sister."

"Oh." I try to hide my surprise and just keep walking. "Well, if you're looking for your sister, she's right up there."

No way I want to get into a conversation with Madison's sister. I mean, someone had to teach Madison everything she knows. Madison probably somehow charmed Mr. Jacobi into letting her sister chaperone us, even though it's a total conflict of interest.

"So, where are we going, anyway?" Madison's sister asks,

obviously not getting the picture that she should be hanging out with Madison and not me.

And, wow. Talk about not being prepared for your job.

"The elementary school," I say, even though it's pretty obvious, since the whole group is turning into the long, winding driveway. The long, winding driveway that has a huge stone sign in front of it that says STONERIDGE ELEMENTARY.

"For what?"

"To tutor kids in math!" I say, exasperated. "Did you not pay attention when you were asked to chaperone?" I realize it's probably not the best idea to antagonize Madison's sister, especially if she's going to be in some kind of position of authority, but I can't help it.

Plus if she gives a really bad report about me to Mr. Jacobi, maybe he'll kick me out of the program, and then I'll have no choice but to not do this anymore. I glance at Madison's sister out of the corner of my eye, wondering if she's the type to tattle. She doesn't seem like she is. She seems like she's totally unconcerned with everything that's going on. She's not even wearing a coat, and it's, like, forty degrees out.

"What do you mean, chaperoning?" she asks. "No one said anything about being a chaperone!" She looks kind of panicked.

"Relax," I say, rolling my eyes. "You don't have to freak

out. I'm sure it's not going to be that much work." God. These spoiled rich kids are so entitled.

"Oh." She relaxes. "So it's not like rolling a fireball up a hill for eternity or something?"

I shake my head. "What are you talking about, rolling a fireball up a hill?"

"You know." She lowers her voice. "*H-E* double hockey sticks?" She has this really scared look on her face. What is up with this girl? Madison's sister obviously has a screw loose.

"Yeah, well, I'm sure you'll be fine." I start to quicken my pace a little bit. Time to get away from this lunatic.

"Hey!" she calls as I start to walk away from her. "What's your name?"

I think about giving her a fake one, but then I realize she's probably going to find out my name soon enough anyway. I sigh. "Kendall," I say.

She nods. "Kendall. Pretty name." I look at her for any signs that she's being fake or sarcastic, but she's not. "I'm Lily."

"Lily," I say. "Okay, sounds good!" I turn around and start to walk back toward the front of our group, but she calls my name.

I turn around. "Yes?"

"Can I ask you one more question?"

"I guess." We're almost at the door to the elementary

school now, and I'm this close to getting away from her.

She tugs on a strand of her hair and looks around, confused. "How come nobody can hear me but you?"

Great. Lily's a ghost. How, how, *how* does this keep happening to me? Seriously, until recently, none of the ghosts I saw had any personal connection to me. Now, in the span of, like, a month, I've attracted Brandon's mom, and now Madison's sister. (And Micah's sister too, but she doesn't really count. I mean, I found Micah because of her, not the other way around.)

I have a vague memory of Ellie telling me something about Madison Baker's sister dying. But that was a few weeks before school started, and for some reason I just assumed Madison's sister was a lot older than us. Like, twenty-five or something. Plus Madison wasn't really on my radar at that time—I didn't have a crush on Brandon then, so she didn't really have any bearing on my life.

I really should start asking everyone I know about their dead relatives so I can be better prepared for this. Or at least start keeping a list.

"I don't know why no one can hear you but me," I say, turning and walking quickly toward the elementary school. I follow the line of my classmates into the school, letting the warm inside air envelop me like a nice cozy blanket. My new plan is to just ignore Lily. No way I want to get involved with anyone related to Madison Baker. Plus I kind of have no choice. I can't talk to Lily when people are around. No one can hear her. They'll think I'm crazy and talking to myself.

Mr. Jacobi is standing in the lobby, looking down at a clipboard and talking to another teacher, probably from the elementary school. I didn't realize it when I first walked in, probably because I was so distracted by Lily, but there's already a bunch of middle school kids standing around in the lobby. Must be kids from other classes at our school who are also involved in the program.

I look back up toward Mr. Jacobi. Why aren't we getting this show on the road? I really want to get this over with. But he's not showing any signs of being productive. He's just chatting away with the elementary school teacher. She's short and pretty, with long red curls and a fair complexion. Probably he thinks he's going to make a love connection with her. At the expense of his own class.

Lily's in the corner now, frowning as she stands on her tiptoes and looks around. I hope she's looking for her sister and not me. I quickly turn around and get very busy staring at the wall, where a bunch of second graders have hung up their art projects. Hopefully, if I don't meet Lily's eye, she'll get the message that I don't want to be bothered.

Wow. These art projects are actually really good. One of the kids drew a picture of a donkey, and it looks just like a real donkey. Every time I try to draw pictures of animals, I always end up messing up the legs. But this kid really knows how to draw. I look at the name on the bottom. Drawing by Tatiana Shaw. She's probably some kind of seven-year-old art savant or something.

This picture's probably going to be worth millions someday. That's totally how people make big money in the art world. They have an eye for talent, and they snatch up paintings before anyone's ever heard of the artist, and then, when the artist gets big, the buyer sells the paintings and gets rich. That's what Ellie's aunt used to do. Of course, then she ended up making a mistake and sinking all her money into this one artist whose art never really panned out, and she lost everything.

But I'll bet I could get this one really cheap, since the artist is only in second grade. Although I'm not sure pictures of donkeys are really that much in demand. And now that I'm looking at it, this donkey might actually be a horse. It has ears like a donkey, but its height is definitely—

"Yo, girl," someone says, and pulls my hat off my head.

I turn around. Micah.

"Oh," I say, surprised. "It's you."

"Yup. It's me." He grins.

"I didn't realize you'd be here," I say. "I didn't know eighth graders were participating in this program."

"Only some of us." He grins and wiggles his eyebrows

up and down, like he's letting me in on some kind of secret. Then he leans in and says, "I'm actually very good at math. But a lot of people don't realize that because I'm so good-looking."

I stare at him blankly, wondering if he's joking. He doesn't *seem* like he's joking, but he can't seriously think it's okay for him to claim he's so good-looking that a lot of people don't know he's smart, can he? Like, on what planet is that acceptable? Not to mention, you don't even have to be good at math to be here. I mean, I'm here. So the standards are pretty low.

"Well, that's great." I reach out and take my hat out of his hands and shove it into my pocket. Then I stand on my tiptoes and pretend to be looking around for someone. Lily's still in the corner, and when she sees me, she waves. I quickly look past her, wondering what would happen if I just pretended I couldn't see or hear her, like everyone else.

"Do you know if there's going to be snacks here?" Micah's asking. He's rummaging through his bag. A bunch of papers come tumbling out and fall onto the floor. A kid walking by steps on one of them, leaving a huge dirty footprint on the front.

Micah doesn't seem to notice. I sigh, then bend down and pick up the papers.

"Thanks," he says, not even bothering to look as he

crumples them and shoves them back into his bag. "There it is!" he says a minute later. He pulls out a half-empty bag of Cheetos and offers me one. "Want?"

"No." They definitely look stale.

"Heeeeyyy," an annoyingly familiar voice trills. "What are you guys doing?"

"Hey, Madison," Micah says, sounding happy to see her. Which makes no sense. Who could be happy to see Madison? "Want some Cheetos?"

"No, thanks." She smiles and twirls a lock of hair around her finger. She definitely wears extensions. There's no way her hair curls that way naturally. It's too perfect. I search her head for signs of clip-ins, but there are none. Does Madison have real hair extensions? The kind people pay thousands of dollars for?

Because that would be ridiculous. My dad won't even let me use the clip-in ones. He says they're unnecessary. I keep trying to tell him that most things in this world are unnecessary. And that if he's that worried about it, maybe he should stop drinking so much bottled water.

"So what are you two lovebirds doing over here?" Madison asks, giving me and Micah a knowing smirk. "Wanted to get some alone time, did you?"

"Yup," Micah says, putting his arm around me. "Just getting a little alone time."

My mouth drops. Is Micah delusional? Why is he putting

his arm around me? And what is he talking about, getting some alone time? We are not. He just came up to me while I was looking at a picture of a donkey/horse. Plus as far as he knows, I have a boyfriend.

"That's so cute," Madison says. "So are you guys, like, a thing now?"

"No," I say at the same time Micah says, "Not officially."

He pulls me closer to him. Wow. He actually has very strong arms. I wonder if he's been working out. It's really a shame that he's kind of crazy, because he's very good-looking. Not as good-looking as Brandon, of course.

"Kendall just broke up with Brandon," Micah says sadly. "She's going to need some time to process that."

"How did *you* know I broke up with Brandon?" I ask.

"It's all over school," he says.

"It is?" How is it all over school? I didn't even realize anyone in school knew that me and Brandon were together, and now people are talking about us breaking up? I know it's totally shallow, but I get a little thrill thinking about it.

Madison's smirk is still playing on her perfectly glossed lips. She's probably the one who told everyone that me and Brandon broke up. I resist the urge to glare at her.

"You okay, Kendall?" she asks. "You seem a little sad." She juts out her bottom lip, like she's doing an impression of me. Which is crazy. I'm not even pouting.

"I'm not sad," I say.

"Are you sure?" She looks at me suspiciously. She wants me to have some kind of meltdown so I'll confess that I miss Brandon and she can feel all happy about my misery. Well! She has another thing coming.

"I'm sure. I'm really happy to be here with Micah." I try to think of something I can do to prove it, so I reach into my pocket and pull out my hat, then pull it down over Micah's head. "Ha-ha!" I say. "You're wearing my hat!" It's supposed to be playful and flirty, but I must not be a very good flirt, because the whole thing just seems kind of weird.

"Ew," Micah says, pulling it off and handing it back to me. "No, thank you."

"Ha-ha," I try again. But I'm kind of insulted. Why doesn't Micah want to wear my hat? It's perfectly clean. And so is my hair. I just washed it this morning.

"Hello, students!" Mr. Jacobi says from the other side of the lobby. "If I can have your attention, please!"

Everyone kind of ignores him, probably because most people can't hear him. The end of the day is the worst time to try to get kids to focus. We're all too excited about finally being out of school.

"Hello, people!" Mr. Jacobi practically screams. "Can we all please quiet down? It's never too early to start setting a good example for the young children we're going to be tutoring." He shakes his head and looks at the teacher standing next to him, the one with red hair he was talking to earlier. She gives him a sympathetic look, like she's glad she's spending her days taking care of little kids and teaching them to draw donkeys, instead of having to hang out with the likes of us.

Finally we all settle down.

Micah moves closer to me.

Like, uncomfortably close.

I'm about to move away, but then I see Madison watching us from the other side of the room. So I stay where I am.

"Excuse me," Lily whispers, coming up behind me. "I'm really sorry to bother you, but can you please tell me why you're the only one who can hear me?"

I put a blank look on my face and try to concentrate on what Mr. Jacobi is saying. Although, it's hard to focus when he's just going on and on about how he's expecting us all to represent our school in the best light possible and blah, blah, blah.

"Hello?" Lily asks. "Kendall? I understand that I'm dead and all, but how come no one else can hear me?" She's not being rude about it. She sounds legitimately bewildered. When I don't answer her, she wanders away, back over to where Madison is standing. I watch her go, saying a silent thanks that she's leaving me alone.

But as I move my eyes back up toward where Mr. Jacobi's standing, I catch Brandon's gaze. He's standing next to Jason

Fields and looking back to where I'm standing, obviously not paying any attention to what Mr. Jacobi is saying. My breath catches in my chest, and everything kind of stops, almost like the world switches over to slow motion. He's wearing his gray-and-navy jacket, the one that makes him look like an Abercrombie model. Or at least a Disney star.

There's a slightly sad expression on his face, and for a second I think maybe he's going to come over and try to talk to me. Which I know is silly, since Mr. Jacobi is talking to us and everyone is actually being quiet for once, and if Brandon started coming over to me right now, it would definitely cause a disturbance.

But Brandon isn't looking away, so I give him a tiny smile, and he starts to raise his hand, like maybe he's going to wave. My heart thumps in my chest, and warmth rushes to my cheeks. If Brandon is waving at me, maybe he's not as mad as I thought he was.

So I make my smile a little bigger, and he raises his hand a little more. My heart starts dancing around. If he waves, what am I going to do? Definitely I should wave back, but then what? Am I going to try to talk to him after tutoring? Should I text him? Should I—

At that moment, for some stupid reason, Micah reaches out and grabs my hand. Like, he is *holding* my hand.

And Brandon sees Micah do it. And then Brandon quickly moves his eyes back to Mr. Jacobi.

I drop Micah's hand like it's an explosive.

Great. A chance to maybe make some progress with Brandon, and what happens? It gets wrecked.

And the worst part of it all is that Madison Baker is watching the whole thing with a satisfied smile on her face.

The rest of the after-school meeting is a ridiculous waste of time. We're supposed to get assigned students and peer groups, but Mr. Jacobi apparently got his wires crossed with the red-haired elementary school teacher and she didn't have anything ready, so nothing gets accomplished except for all of us standing around getting lectured about being good role models.

The afternoon goes from bad to worse when I get home and my dad informs me that we (me, him, and his girlfriend, Cindy, are now apparently a "we," according to my dad—how cozy) are going to Best Buy to pick out a TV for my room.

"Why do I need a TV for my room?" I ask as my dad and I drive to meet Cindy at the mall. I'm being a brat. Of course I want a TV for my room. Who wouldn't want a TV for their room? Watching *Pretty Little Liars* and *The Vampire Diaries* on my laptop is all well and good, but let's face it—there's no substitute for Ian Somerhalder on the big screen.

But up until now my dad has been anti-TV-in-my-room,

believing that I'm going to hole up all day, watching movies and refusing to interact with society.

So if I want to watch TV, I have to do it in the living room. Which is probably why I'm suddenly now being allowed to have a TV in my room. Obviously, Cindy and my dad want the downstairs TV all to themselves. They want to, like, marginalize me to my room so they can hold hands on the couch while they watch sappy Nicholas Sparks movies.

Not that they have to worry. Since I have no friends and no boyfriend, I'll be spending all of my time moping around my room anyway. My dad will probably blame it on the new TV and think that his worst fears are coming true.

"I just think it's time for you to have one," my dad says.

I roll my eyes as I get out of the car. Maybe after we're done picking out the TV, he'll let me go look at hair accessories. Maybe doing my hair in some fun new whimsical styles will make my mood more fun and whimsical.

Cindy's waiting for us outside the store. She's wearing this really nice camel-colored long wool coat that's extremely stylish, but for some reason she has paired it with mom jeans.

"Hey, Cindy," I say.

"Hi, Kendall." She gives me a big smile, like she's superhappy to see me. "I like your shirt."

"Thanks," I say. "I like your coat."

"You do?" She beams. "It's new."

We walk inside and are immediately accosted by a salesperson wearing a nametag that says ROBBI. There's an outline of an *E* after that, which obviously means his name is Robbie and a letter fell off somewhere.

"Hello," he says. "And what are you shopping for today?"

"We're just looking," my dad says firmly, and I roll my eyes. My dad hates salespeople. Seriously, he totally refuses to ask for help with anything. When his doctor put him on a low-cholesterol diet and gave him a list of supplements that might help, he wandered around Whole Foods for half an hour before I talked to an employee without him noticing. It's totally ridiculous.

"We're looking for a TV," I say now. If I'm going to be getting a TV, then I'm definitely going to need something high-end. If I'm going to be stuck in my room with no friends, eating my way through boxes of peanut butter cups, then I should at least be able to do it in high-def style.

"What size?" Robbie asks. "And do you like LCD or plasma?"

"LCD for sure," a voice says behind me. "Plasma's got a better picture, but the tubes always blow out, and then you have to replace them, and I honestly doubt your dad's going to want do that."

"Thanks," I say automatically and turn around, expecting to see another Best Buy employee. But it's not a Best Buy employee. It's Lily. She's peering at a display of heart rate monitors. "Wouldn't it be hilarious if I put one of these on?" she asks, trying to touch them. But of course her hand just goes right through the display case. "Can you imagine?" She throws her head back and laughs. "You know, because I'm dead?" She laughs again.

"Who are you talking to?" my dad asks.

"Uh, Robbie, of course," I say.

"But he asked you what kind of TV we wanted. There was nothing to thank him for." My dad peers at Robbie like he's some kind of con man instead of a college kid who's probably working for minimum wage and just wants us to buy a TV so he can go on his break or whatever.

"I want an LCD," I say. "That way we won't have to keep replacing the bulbs."

My dad looks at me in surprise.

"What?" I say defensively. "Just because I'm a girl, I can't know about electronics?"

"No," my dad says. "Not because you're a girl. But because you've never showed any interest in anything technological before."

"That's such a lie," I say. "Who's the one who set up the wireless printer?"

"You set up the wireless printer?" Cindy asks. "That's amazing!"

I can't tell if she's being nice or condescending. I decide to believe she's being nice. "Thanks," I say, beaming.

"Older people are so impressed with technology," Lily muses. "Of course, I really shouldn't be making fun of old people. They're old and I'm dead, so honestly, they're better off than I am." She sighs and continues to look at the heart rate monitors.

She has a very good point. She actually seems kind of nice. Maybe I judged her too harshly just because she's Madison Baker's sister. Maybe Lily's the nice one. So I probably shouldn't judge Lily just because her sister is a brat.

Oh, well. It's really not my concern anyway. Poor Lily is going to just have to find someone else to help her move on. I've decided I'm out of the ghost business for the foreseeable future.

"So here are our LCD TVs," Robbie says, bringing us over to a section of the store and pointing to them with a flourish. All the TVs are tuned to SportsCenter. How lame.

"Can I turn the channel?" I ask.

"Be my guest."

Robbie hands me the remote, and I turn to ABC Family, where they're showing a rerun of a *Vampire Diaries* episode. Love it! I can just imagine snuggling up in my bed, watching this on the big screen.

"Now, don't think we're going to be buying any kind of

protection plan," my dad tells Robbie. "I read online that those things are rip-offs."

"Okay," Robbie says warily.

"Dad, you don't have to be rude about it," I say, giving Robbie what I hope is a friendly smile.

"I'll tell you what's rude," my dad says. "Trying to get people to part with their hard-earned cash for something they're not going to use." He glares at Robbie again. Jeez. Talk about misplacing your anger.

I look to Cindy for help, but she's just nodding along with my dad while she stares at the television screen. "What's this actor's name?" she asks.

"Ian Somerhalder."

She gets a dreamy little smile on her face. Ew. I think Cindy likes what she sees.

"Don't look so freaked out," Lily whispers to me as she floats down the aisle. "She's old, not blind."

"Anyway," my dad says. "We don't want to be here all day, so let us know what the best-rated TV is and then I'll google it on my phone to make sure you're not being deceptive."

"Why didn't you just google it before you came in here?" Robbie asks sweetly. "Then you wouldn't have to worry about whether or not I was telling the truth."

Wow. Robbie seemed so sedate, and now he's getting smart with my dad. That's definitely not going to go over well.

My dad's lips set in a firm line, the same kind of line they get when he's mad at me. He opens his mouth to say something, but before he can, his cell phone rings.

He looks down at the caller ID, and a look of surprise breaks out on his face.

"I'm sorry," he says. "I have to take this."

It's probably one of his construction clients. Hopefully, a really demanding one who's having some kind of complicated problem that's going to take a long time to fix.

He hurries out of the store.

"What do you think of this one, Cindy?" I ask, not because I really value her opinion but because I need to break her out of her Ian Somerhalder daze.

"Ian Summerfield," Cindy says, watching the screen.

"Somerhalder," I correct.

"Is he in anything else?"

"I think he was in *Lost*."

"Lost!" Her eyes brighten. "I've been meaning to watch that show. Do they have it on Netflix?"

"Um, I'm not sure." Wow, she must really be in love with Ian Somerhalder. And now she's getting all excited because she'll be able to watch *Lost* to get her fix. I mean, how would she really explain to my dad that she wants to watch *The Vampire Diaries*?

"Ian Somerhalder is way too skinny," Lily says. "He's definitely nowhere near as cute as Channing Tatum."

"Agreed," I say, before I remember I'm not supposed to be talking to her.

"So!" I say, flipping through the channels. Obviously, if I want to get Cindy's opinion, I'm going to have to get Ian Somerhalder's face off the screen.

"Oh!" she says, seemingly startled. "Why did you change it?"

"Probably because you were drooling over that guy on television," Robbie says, shaking his head. "All the girls want Ian Somerhalder. My girlfriend is obsessed with that guy. It's annoying."

"Aw," I say. "I'm sure she thinks you're just as good-looking as he is." Robbie has frizzy hair and a little bit of acne, but beauty is only skin deep. I'm sure his girlfriend loves the way he looks. Otherwise, why would she be with him?

"No, she doesn't," Robbie grumbles.

"How do you know?" I ask. *Click, click, click.* I switch through the channels fast, trying to get a look at as many different programs as I can. I think it's probably important to be diverse when it comes to figuring out picture quality.

"Because she says, 'Wow, you really aren't as good-looking as Ian Somerhalder.'"

"That's really rude," Lily says. She's sitting on the floor of the store now, watching some kind of volleyball game playing on one of the screens on the bottom shelf.

"That's really rude," I echo. "It might be time for you to get a new girlfriend."

"Yes," Cindy chimes in. "If someone isn't treating you with the respect you deserve, it's time to find someone who will."

She sounds very wise. I wonder if it's because of her and my dad. There was this whole big scandal involving him not wanting to tell me about the two of them being together. So he kept the relationship a secret, and Cindy got super-annoyed by it. And so then she got offered this job in Virginia, and she threatened to take it.

That's why my dad bought her that promise ring—to, like, prove his love to her. And it seemed to have worked, because from what I can tell, they're happier than ever. Well. As long as Cindy never meets Ian Somerhalder.

"I *was* thinking it might be fun to try out the single life," Robbie says. He watches as a girl walks by, her long blond hair swishing as she goes.

When did this trip turn into some kind of counseling session for Robbie's love life? I'm sure he's a nice guy, but priorities, people.

"Yes, well, I'm sure the single life will be fun," I say. Not. I've been single for, like, a day, and I already realize how bad it sucks. Not only am I single and without a boyfriend, I'm single and without a best friend.

Thinking about Ellie starts to depress me, and I feel a warm tingle at the back of my eyes. I look down at the remote in my hand and try to keep myself from crying.

"You okay?" Lily asks. "Why are you crying?"

I obviously can't tell her, but it's nice of her to ask. I wonder what she would do if she knew that part of the reason my life is such a mess is because of her dumb sister. After all, if Madison hadn't told Brandon that I liked Micah, Brandon wouldn't have been so suspicious, and maybe he wouldn't have been so upset when he saw me and Micah at the bowling alley together. And then I wouldn't have told him that I could see ghosts, in an effort to make sure he wasn't mad at me anymore.

"Whatever," I say, taking a deep breath in through my nose and letting it out through my mouth. "I think we should get this one." I point at the TV I've been watching. "Let's wrap it up."

"Um, okay," Robbie says. He looks a little startled. Probably he's not used to people making such quick decisions.

"Shouldn't you ask your father if the price is okay?" Cindy pipes up and asks.

I stand on my tiptoes and look toward the front of the store. Of course, now that I'm ready to get out of here, my dad's nowhere to be found.

"This TV is very reasonably priced," Robbie says. It's definitely the wrong thing to say, since apparently Cindy shares my dad's belief that salespeople are the devil. She glares at him suspiciously.

"Maybe we should try calling my dad," I say, and pull my cell phone out of my purse. "And let him know we're ready."

"I don't know," Cindy says. "What if he's on a business call?"

"Then he just won't answer," I say.

I push the call button and listen as the phone rings. But then I catch sight of my dad walking into the store.

He doesn't look happy. Probably he's dealing with some kind of work emergency. Good. Maybe he won't be in the mood to ask a ton of questions and he'll just let me get the TV I already picked out.

Robbie switches through the channels on another TV before settling on a boxing match. He has morphed from pretending to do his job to pretty much not doing it. And if he gets testy with my dad, we're never going to get out of here.

"Oh, there's your father," Cindy says, deciding to state the obvious. She fluffs up her hair, like my dad didn't just see her a few minutes ago. Her hair looks exactly the same. In fact, her hair always looks exactly the same. She insists on wearing it in this totally crazy beehive, with poufy bangs.

Maybe I should offer to take her to the salon for a haircut. But obviously not the one Micah's mom owns. Actually, I don't even think they do haircuts there. I'm not sure what they do besides manicures.

"Hey," I say once my dad's within earshot. "I'm going

to get this one, okay? It's supposed to be a very good deal." I point to the little card that's perched near the television, which shows that the TV has a user rating of four and a half out of five stars on the Best Buy website.

He narrows his eyes at me, and I know what he's going to say. He's going to say that reviews on websites are usually bought and paid for by the companies that own the product, and that you have to look at a third-party source, like *Consumer Reports*. But really, who has time for that?

I sigh and resign myself to being in this store for a long time.

"You should just let your dad pick out the one he wants you to have, and then you can approve it," Lily offers. "That's what I always do whenever my parents are going to buy me something."

Wow. That's actually a really good idea. Turns out Lily is nicer and smarter than her sister. Although Madison's not really dumb. Which is why it's totally ridiculous that she pretends to need help on her homework just so she can talk to Brandon. It's so transparent. Plus think about what it's doing for feminism. Pretending to be stupid so that a boy can help you? She should be a cautionary tale.

"So," I say. "We can get this one, or you can just pick out—"

"Kendall," my dad says, his voice stern. "Where were you this weekend?"

"This weekend?" I frown. It takes me a second to realize what he's talking about, and when I do, my stomach twists into a knot. "I told you," I say, getting really busy looking at another TV. "I was at Ellie's house on Friday night."

It's a lie, of course. I wasn't at Ellie's house. I was at Micah's house. And then at the bowling alley. But obviously I couldn't tell my dad that. My dad was already freaked out that I have (had) a boyfriend. There was no way he was going to be cool with me hanging out with some other guy he'd never even met. So I told him I was at Ellie's.

"Maybe I should get a Blu-ray player too," I say in an effort to distract. Everyone knows Blu-ray players are a waste, since everything's online now anyway. Who wants to have to buy a bunch of discs? "I don't care how much they cost. I really want one!" I stamp my foot, like maybe I'm about to start having a tantrum. A fake one, of course.

"Kendall," my dad says. "You were not at Ellie's house this weekend."

"Yes, I was," I say. The knot in my stomach tightens. Who was that on the phone? Someone telling him where I really was? Micah's mom, maybe? But why would she do that?

Could it have been Ellie on the phone? Calling my dad just so she could get me in trouble? I know she's mad at me, but to go out of her way to do something so evil is definitely taking it a little too far.

"I don't know what you're talking about," I try feebly, but I already know it's over. My dad knows I was at Micah's. And now I'm going to be in a lot, lot, *lot* of trouble.

Oh, well. At least he doesn't know I went to see my mom.

"What I'm talking about," my dad says, "is that you took a bus to go see your mother."

Chapter 5

Well. Talk about your worst-case scenarios. I mean, lying to my dad about hanging out with a boy from school while his mom was right in the other room is one thing. Lying to my dad about taking a two-hour bus trip *by myself* and using the emergency credit card he gave me to purchase the ticket so that I could go see my mom, who abandoned me when I was a baby, is another thing altogether.

Needless to say, my dad is mad enough that he's decided I will not be getting a new TV, regardless of what Cindy thinks about me watching TV in the living room with them.

Speaking of Cindy, she seems totally cool about my mom calling my dad. Which is weird. Cindy's always been a little wary of my mom, since I'm pretty sure my dad thinks my mom is the love of his life. Or *was* the love of his life. Whatever. But apparently my dad and Cindy have put all that behind them, because Cindy didn't seem threatened at all. She just kissed my dad's cheek, told him to call her later, and headed for her car.

Anyway, how does my mom have my dad's number? They're supposed to be, like, estranged.

I glance at my dad out of the corner of my eye. We're in the car now, on the way back to our house. At least I think that's where we're going. For all I know he's taking me to a detention center or something. Seriously, I've never seen him this mad before.

Usually he doesn't like to show much emotion. But now he's gripping the steering wheel so hard, his knuckles are turning white. He's actually driving a little fast, too, but something tells me this is definitely not the time to point that out.

We don't talk the whole car ride home.

And when we pull into the driveway, my dad leaves the car running.

I'm not sure if I'm supposed to get out or not, so I just sit there.

A minute ticks by.

Then two.

I never realized how hot it was in this car.

I want to take my coat off, but something about the vibe in here is making it, uh, hard to move.

I cough, hoping to maybe break the tension.

But my dad still doesn't say anything. I glance at him again. He's still holding on to the steering wheel, his knuckles still white.

Finally, I can't take it anymore.

"So should we go inside?" I ask. "Because I could make us hot cocoa or something. And maybe we could have some of that apple pie Cindy made. It's low sugar, so it won't hurt your cholesterol."

My dad stays quiet. I can practically see the steam coming out of his ears.

"Okay," I say, unbuckling my seat belt. "Well, I'm going to go inside. I'll get the stuff ready for pie and cocoa, so if you want to come in—"

"This is completely unacceptable, Kendall," my dad says. "You cannot be going off to see your mother and lying to me about it."

"I didn't *lie* about it," I say, shifting on the seat. "I just didn't tell you where I was."

"You lied," my dad said. "You left me a note saying you were going to be having breakfast with Ellie."

Oh. Right. I forgot about that.

"Well, it was a spur-of-the-moment decision," I say. "I did go to Ellie's, but then—"

"Kendall," he says. "I don't— I'm not—" He takes in a deep breath, and then I see some of his anger fade away.

"Why did you go to see your mom? I understand that you would want to, but why now? And why didn't you talk to me about it?"

I look down at my hands. "I don't know. I just . . ." I think of telling him about the ghosts. Maybe he could help me. Maybe he already knows. But I can't say the words out loud. "It's complicated," I finally say.

He nods. "I know you're at an age when you might be starting to have questions about your mother. I guess I just thought . . ." He sighs.

We sit there in silence for a moment, the only sound the hum of the engine. "Do you and Mom . . . Do you guys talk all the time?" I ask finally.

He shakes his head. "Not all the time. She calls me once in a while, yes."

"How often?"

"Not very. Maybe once a year."

"Since when?"

"Since she left."

"Why didn't you tell me?"

"Because I didn't want you to think . . ." He trails off, but I know what he was about to say . He was going to say that he didn't want me to think it meant that my mom wanted to be a part of my life. "Should we go inside and talk about this?" he asks.

"Not right now." I shake my head. I've changed my

mind. It's too raw. "Can we . . . Can we do it later?"

"Okay." I can see the pain on my dad's face, and I can tell how hard this is for him. Neither one of us moves, and then my dad finally says, "I'm going to go for a drive and clear my head."

"Oh. Okay." I swallow, then reach out and open the car door. "Well, um, drive safe."

I get out and close the car door behind me. I hear my dad pulling out as I head inside.

The house feels empty without my dad. I know most of it is in my mind, because it's not like I've never been home alone before.

I wander around for a little while, not sure what to do with myself.

I fix myself some cookies and milk.

I make myself a ham and cheese sandwich. I nibble on the inside and then throw the crusts away.

I bring my cookies into the living room and flip through the channels on the TV, but there's nothing good on.

"Hey," a voice says softly, and I scream.

It's Lily.

Great.

Why is it that even though I'm feeling lonely, the one person I don't want to see shows up?

"What's wrong?" she asks, sitting down next to me.

"Oh, nothing," I say sarcastically. "Just maybe everyone I ever cared about in my life hates me or is disappointed in me or thinks I might be crazy." I pick up an Oreo and dunk it into my milk angrily. I wait until the chocolate part gets good and mushy before popping it into my mouth.

"I'm sure that's not true," Lily says, like I'm being dramatic.

"Yes, it is."

"You want to talk about it?"

"No." I really don't. And it's not just because she's Madison's sister. It wouldn't matter who she was. I don't want to talk about what's going on, because I'm sick of thinking about Ellie and Brandon and now my dad. I need a distraction. I need to focus on something other than myself. I need to get out of here.

"Come on," I say to Lily. "We're going to the cemetery."

"I love cemeteries," Lily says as we walk across the street. She's surprisingly upbeat for a ghost. I mean, most ghosts are all freaked out about the fact that they're dead, and they get even more freaked out when you bring them to the cemetery. They think they're going to get buried alive or something. Which is pretty funny, since obviously you can't be buried alive when you're already dead. But try telling that to a ghost. They're not logical.

I pull my notebook out of my bag and sit down on my

favorite bench. The days are getting shorter, and it's almost dark out now. It's one of those nights when you can really tell winter is just around the corner. I shiver. I love the fall, but I am so not a winter person. The only good thing about winter is that Ellie and I make this amazing white mocha hot chocolate every morning and drink it out of our thermoses before school. We even have matching snowflake thermoses—hers is maroon, and mine is dark blue.

But now that Ellie's not talking to me, we obviously won't be doing that. I wonder what she'll do with her thermos. It wasn't in the box of stuff she brought over to my house. Maybe she threw it away, or maybe she took a Sharpie and scribbled all over it to get some anger out.

"So," I say to Lily. "Tell me what you remember."

"What do you mean?" Lily pulls on a strand of her hair and sits down on the bench next to me.

I try not to be impatient with her. She's being perfectly nice. It's not her fault I'm in a bad mood because my life is a mess.

"Well, here's how it works," I say, slipping my hair tie off my wrist and pulling my hair into a low ponytail. Then I take my winter hat out of my pocket and put it on. There's no way I can wear my hair back without something covering my ears—it's way too cold. "You're still here, uh, on earth, because you have some kind of unfinished business. So you need to take care of that business, and then you can move on." I really hope she doesn't ask me where it is she's moving on to, because I honestly have no idea.

"Okay." She nods. "So I need to tell you everything I remember, and you'll help me figure out what I need to do to move on?"

"Exactly." She's very smart for a ghost. And she's not trying to fight me on anything, which I really appreciate. The worst is when a ghost shows up with an attitude, trying to act like they know better than I do, or expecting me to do all the work. You'd be surprised at how many of them are like that.

"Okay. Well, I know I *fell* off something," she says. "That's how I died." She closes her eyes. She has the longest lashes I've ever seen. I wonder if they're those new eyelash extensions you can get. If her parents are willing to pay for Madison to have hair extensions, why not eyelash extensions for Lily?

"It think it was a balcony or something," she says. "In my room."

"Wow," I say, writing it down. "That's awful."

"Yeah." She shrugs. "But what are you gonna do? I loved that balcony. I used to go out there all the time to write."

"You're a writer?" I ask, surprised. I've always thought that maybe someday I'll be a writer. I even keep a notebook of ideas I have that could turn into novels.

"Yes," Lily says proudly. "I'd just finished my first novel

a few weeks before I died, and I've written hundreds of poems. Oh, and I've kept a journal since I was five."

"Wow." Lily is actually very impressive. Probably she got all the cool genes in her family, and so by the time Madison came along, she got stuck with the ones that make you snobby and stuck-up and cause you to want to steal other people's boyfriends.

"Okay, so you fell off a balcony," I say. "In your room. Anything else you can remember?"

She closes her eyes. "Yes." She nods. "I know that whatever it is I need to take care of has to do with my mom. And that it also has to do with something in my room." She bites her lip and concentrates. "But that's all I can remember."

She seems disappointed, so I rush to reassure her. "No, no," I say. "That's great. You're doing great."

"I am?"

"Yeah. You'd be surprised how many ghosts can't remember anything."

She blinks in confusion. "I'm a ghost?"

"Yeah. I mean, not like the kind you see in movies or anything. You're not white and floaty." I peer at her. "Although, you are a little bit, uh, see-through."

She looks down at herself and fingers the bottom of the long violet-colored sweater she's wearing. Then she picks her arm up and watches it trail through the air.

"But I wouldn't get too caught up in the semantics of it,"

I say. "I mean, 'ghost' is just a word. Your life is really what you make of it." That last part doesn't make much sense, since obviously she doesn't have a life anymore, at least not here on earth, but she must get the gist of what I'm saying, because she nods.

"Okay," she says. "I guess."

"So," I say, looking down at my notebook. "It's good that you remember so much, but the hard part for me is going to be getting into your room."

She nods. "So, what? You have to, like, break into my house or something?"

"No." I take a deep breath. "I need to somehow get invited over there."

"Well, that's easy," she says. "Don't you know my sister?"

I consider this. Obviously I do know Madison. But now's definitely not the time to tell Lily about the, uh, complicated history Madison and I share. The poor girl has been through enough. Plus she obviously doesn't know her sister is a big brat. If she did, she wouldn't be expecting me to go over there and somehow get invited in.

"Yeah," I say slowly. "I know Madison."

"Great!" Lily's face brightens. Her smile is very pretty. "Are you friends with her? Maybe she'll invite you over. Madison loves having people over." She rolls her eyes. "It used to be so annoying, her and her friends playing their music while I was trying to study. And now I kind of miss it."

"Right," I say. "Um . . ." I think about it. Madison *did* give me her phone number. So I guess, technically, I could send her a text or something and try to get invited over to her house. Then, once I'm there, I could try to sneak into Lily's room, have a look around, and see if there's anything there that could help me. On the other hand, the last thing I want to do is spend time with Madison Baker.

Plus what if I call her and she's with Brandon? Could you imagine how horrible that would be?

"You should call her," Lily says, sounding even happier than she did a second ago.

"Sure," I say, shutting my notebook. "Or maybe tomorrow I can talk to her in school."

"Oh." Lily's face falls, and she pulls on one of her long curls. "I thought maybe we'd be getting started today. I mean, I just thought, if you guys are friends . . ."

I sigh, then look over my shoulder. The only thing waiting for me at home is an empty house, where I'd probably end up in my room, counting down the seconds until my dad got back so we could have some big, horrible conversation about me lying to him. And let's face it, this isn't going to be the normal how-could-you-have-lied-to-me-and-gone-somewhere-without-telling-me conversation. This is going to be a long, emotional why-did-you-go-see-your-mother conversation.

And I know I said I was done with this whole helping-ghosts thing, but Lily seems so nice. Plus if I'm going to have to somehow get myself invited over to Madison's house, shouldn't I just get it over with?

I pull my phone out of my purse and scroll down to Madison's phone number.

I click call and cross my fingers that she doesn't answer. At least then it will be out of my hands and I won't have a choice about what to do. The decision will be made for me.

One ring . . . two . . . Madison's definitely one of those people who always have their phones with them. I've seen her texting constantly when our teachers aren't looking. She's also probably one of those people who look at the caller ID and decide whether or not they want to take the call. I can just imagine her looking down at the phone, seeing it's me, then rolling her eyes and sending me to voice mail. She probably thinks I'm—

"Hello?"

"Oh," I say, surprised she actually answered. "Hi."

"Who is this?" she asks, obviously just to be snotty. She knows it's me.

"It's Kendall," I say. At this point I want to hang up, but really, there's no turning back now.

"Oh, Kendall," she says. "Hi." There's a bunch of talking and laughing in the background.

"Are you busy?" I ask, hoping she says yes.

"No," she says. "Well, I mean, I'm always busy doing

something. Right now I'm at the mall, picking out an assortment of boots for winter."

"Oh. Well, if you need to call me back, then—"

"I don't need to call you back," she says. "I'm pretty much done. They have nothing knee-high here, which is a total disappointment."

I have no idea what she's talking about, but I feel like she wants some kind of reaction out of me, so I say, "Wow, that sucks," in what I hope is a sympathetic tone.

"Yeah," she says. Then she lowers her voice, like we're old friends and she wants to tell me a secret. "So what's going on? Do you need to talk?"

"Talk?" I repeat, confused. And then I realize she thinks I'm calling her because I'm upset about Brandon, or maybe confused about Micah. I don't want to talk to Madison about Brandon. I really do not want to hear about how they've been hanging out, or anything he said about how much he hates me, or if he told her I told him I could see ghosts. But if I want to make sure I get invited over to her house so that I can get into Lily's room, then I'm probably going to have to at least give her a little something.

"Yeah," Madison says, sounding annoyed. "You know, about all your emotional problems."

"They're not emotional problems," I say before I can stop myself. Next to me, Lily frowns and looks at me in confusion.

"Well, kind of they are," Madison says. "They're really hard issues to deal with. I mean, if the love of my life broke up with me, I'd be a total basket case." You can tell from her tone that she doesn't think that would ever happen to her.

"Yeah," I say, hating myself a little as I say the words, "it *has* been really hard. And it *would* be nice to have someone to talk to."

"So talk," she says. "I'm listening." Which isn't even true, because a second later I can hear her telling a salesperson to wrap up the boots she wants, and that she'll be paying for them with a credit card.

"It's not really something I want to get into over the phone," I say. "I'd rather talk in person."

She sighs, like she can't believe she's actually going to have to hang out with me to get some gossip. But she must decide it's worth it, because she says, "Okay, I get it. After I'm done buying my boots, I'll come over."

Someone mumbles something in the background, and then Madison says, "No, Maura, you're going home."

She must mean Maura Dohnson, one of her little minions. Apparently Madison's going to ditch Maura to hang out with me. Probably Maura's used to it, though. I mean, if she's friends with Madison, I'm sure that's not the worst thing she's been through.

"Um, well, you can't come over here," I say. "My dad's not letting me have friends over right now."

"Because of your emotional problems?"

"Exactly." I roll my eyes. Lily's giving me a what-is-she-saying look, but it's way too complicated to get into, especially with a ghost.

"Fine," Madison says. "You can come to my house."

"Great." I give Lily a thumbs-up sign, and she claps her hands.

"I'll text you the address," Madison says. "But give me, like, forty-five minutes to get home."

"No prob," I say, then click off.

"Wow," Lily says. "That was awesome. You're a really good liar."

I'm actually kind of a terrible liar. But I don't want her to lose confidence in me. I mean, we've just gotten our first victory. "Lily," I say, "you have no idea."

Chapter 6

Turns out Madison didn't have to worry about me waiting forty-five minutes to get to her house, because it takes me a good forty minutes just to bike over there. I'm probably not supposed to be riding my bike so far in the dark, but since my dad's not home, I just leave him a note letting him know I'm at my friend Madison's house. I mean, it doesn't even really matter. A little bike ride at seven o'clock is probably not going to rate high on the list of things he's upset with me about, when I already took a bus halfway across the state to see my mom.

I thought for sure Madison would live in one of those neighborhoods filled with big, sprawling McMansions, the kind of houses that all look the same and have long, winding driveways and street names like Cider Cove Circle and Pashmina Glen.

But Madison's neighborhood looks pretty normal. Yes, the houses are big, but not, like, over-the-top crazy or anything.

"I miss this house," Lily says wistfully as she hops off my bike. She could have just floated alongside me, and she did for part of the way, but then she started goofing around, sitting on my handlebars and pretending she was catching a ride. It was pretty funny, actually.

I climb the cobblestone steps and ring the doorbell.

Madison makes me wait, like, two minutes before she finally answers the door.

"Oh," she says when she sees me standing on the top step. "You're here." She sounds all surprised, like she didn't just invite me over less than an hour ago.

Then suddenly she grabs my hand and drags me up the stairs. "My friend's here and we're going upstairs," she yells over her shoulder, I guess to her parents.

She herds me into her room, then lets go of my hand and shuts the door behind us.

Lily gets caught out in the hallway. "Wow," she says as she floats through the door. "How rude."

I smile. It's kind of funny, Lily calling her own sister rude.

"What are you smiling about?" Madison asks. She tilts her head and looks at me. "Is something funny?"

"No." I shake my head and then sit down on her bed. She has an aqua-and-black-striped comforter that's very cool. "I was just remembering this joke I heard."

"Whatever," Madison says. She sits down next to me and starts unzipping her boots. They're the kind that zip all the way up to your knee, the kind of boots my dad would never let me wear in a million billion years. She's wearing them over a pair of patterned gray tights. Actually, now that I think about it, Madison's wearing a completely different outfit from the one she wore to school. I guess going boot shopping calls for a change of clothes.

"I like your boots," I say. "Are they new?"

"No." She doesn't offer any more information, just pulls off her boots and drops them onto the floor with a thunk.

"So," she says, turning to me. And then she takes my hand in hers. "Are you okay? How are you holding up?"

"I'm fine," I say, before remembering I called her and told her I was having a hard time. "I mean, considering all I've been through."

She nods and pats my hand. "I can only imagine. So, what's the deal?"

"Well, it's just really hard," I say. I rack my brains, trying to come up with some salacious details Madison might find interesting. "I mean, Micah is so trying to be my boyfriend, and it's just, I don't really want a boyfriend right now."

Madison frowns. Obviously she doesn't like this. She

probably wanted me to be all upset about Brandon. She stands up, opens her top dresser drawer, and pulls out a long gauzy scarf, then wraps it around her neck. "What about Brandon?" she asks.

"Brandon?"

"Yeah." She arranges the scarf around her neck and then turns this way and that, admiring herself in the full-length mirror. "Aren't you upset that he broke up with you?"

"No," I say. "Because I broke up with him, remember?" Isn't that what I just told her in math today? I'm starting to get to the point where I can't remember my own lies. Which is very dangerous, especially around someone like Madison.

"Whatever." She sighs and then pulls the scarf off her neck. "This scarf makes me look washed out." She tosses it over to me. "You can have it." She beams, like she's done something totally generous instead of just giving me a scarf that she thinks makes her look horrible.

"Um, thanks," I say. I pick it up. Madison's looking at me like she's waiting for me to do or say something else, so after a moment I wrap it around my neck.

"Cute scarf," Lily says, nodding in approval.

I stand up and look at myself in the mirror. It *is* a pretty cute scarf. I don't know what Madison was talking about, that it washes her out. This scarf could not wash anyone out. I touch the material. It's silky and smooth and slips through my fingers like buttery, shimmery, beautiful goodness. This is not a scarf that came from Old Navy or the Gap. This is a scarf that came from somewhere expensive. I wonder if it would be really rude of me to check the label. If I can adjust the scarf on my neck, then maybe I can check the tag without Madison noticing.

"Here!" she says. "These are the perfect earrings to go with that."

She pulls a pair of glittery hoops out of her jewelry box and hands them to me.

"Thanks," I say, putting them on. She's right. They look perf with the scarf.

"I was going to say you can borrow them," she says, choosing a pair of small diamond studs for herself. I wonder if they're real, like her hair extensions. "But they look so good on you that you can just keep them."

"Wow," I say. "Thanks." I'm not being sarcastic—it's really nice of her to give me this beautiful scarf and these beautiful earrings. At the same time, I'm not stupid. Obviously she's trying to suck up to me so that I'll let my guard down and tell her stuff about Brandon.

"So did Brandon ever mention me?" She's pulling a brush through her hair now. "Sit," she commands, pointing to the spot next to her on the vanity bench.

I sit. Hmmm. This is very weird, being in Madison Baker's room, sitting next to her at her vanity and watching as she puts makeup on. Wow. Very bright makeup.

"Here," she says, handing me an eye brush and a big palette of makeup. "Do your eyes."

"Oh. Um, okay."

"So did he?"

"Did he what?"

She sighs, like she can't believe how stupid I am for not being able to keep up with the conversation. "Did Brandon ever mention me to you?"

"Um, I don't think so." I wonder what color eye shadow would look good with this scarf. I settle on a smoky silvery blue and hope that if I go easy on it, it won't make me look like a clown. My grandma always said the trick with makeup is to make it seem like you're not wearing any.

Obviously, Madison doesn't agree with this, since she's piling on the purple eye shadow. Somehow it works on her, though. Her makeup always looks flawless. She should become one of those girls who give makeup tutorials on YouTube.

"Are you sure?" she asks now. "Because I have a feeling he likes me."

My skin gets all tingly.

"Who's Brandon?" Lily asks. She's standing behind us, looking at herself in the mirror. "Cool," she says. "I have a reflection. I didn't think I would. You know, since I'm dead." She tilts her head. "And I'm not as pale as I thought I'd be either."

"You have a feeling Brandon likes you?" I start to carefully swipe some eye shadow across my lid, which doesn't really work so well since my hand is shaking. I try to steady it. No way I want Madison to know I'm freaking out about the thought of Brandon liking her.

"Yeah." She reaches for a plum eyeliner, then draws a perfectly smooth line right above her lashes. "I've always thought he liked me, ever since last year."

"Oh." The fact that she's saying he liked her ever since last year obviously means she thinks he liked her the whole time he and I were together. Which is pretty rude, when you think about it. I'm tempted to rip off my scarf and earrings and throw them at her, then stomp out of the room. But then I remember I have to help Lily. And besides, there's really no sense in rejecting a perfectly good scarf.

"Why?" I ask nonchalantly. "Did he say he likes you?"

"No."

My heart soars.

"But I can tell by the way he looks at me. And how he's always trying to touch my hand, like, for no reason."

My heart sinks.

"Well," I say, "Maybe he—"

"Madison!" a voice calls from downstairs. "Please come and set the table for dinner!"

Madison rolls her eyes, and then she screams, "Mom, I have a friend over!"

"Too bad!" comes the reply. "It's your turn."

Madison sighs. "Be right back." She bounds out of the room. As soon as I'm sure she's down the stairs, I leap up from the vanity bench.

"She's always complaining about doing chores," Lily says, shaking her head. "Half the time she'd con me into doing them for her."

"Where's your room?" I ask, making my way toward the door. I'm not trying to be rude, but we have a limited amount of time to get into Lily's room and see what we can find. Not to mention, I'm really not in the mood for some kind of ridiculous anecdote starring Madison as the lazy sister and Lily as the sister who thinks Madison is so cute and puts up with her layabout ways.

"My room's down the hall, last door on the right," Lily says.

I creep down the hallway. From downstairs I can hear the clink of dishes and silverware hitting the table, so I know it's going to be at least a few minutes before Madison comes back upstairs. Still. Something about this whole thing is a little creepy.

I mean, I'm lurking around in someone else's house. Plus it's dark out now, and for some reason the hall light isn't on. So I'm walking around in a dark, strange house. And when you think about it, what do I *really* know about Madison? Nothing. Being in a few classes with someone doesn't mean you know them. Her family could be crazy. I could find anything behind that door.

Of course, I'm the one who can see ghosts, and now I'm spying and poking around in Madison's house. So probably she's the one who should be nervous.

I take a deep breath and keep going until I get to the last room on the right. There's a sign on the door that says LILY'S ROOM.

"Wait!" Lily says right as I'm about to go in.

I jump. "What?" I whisper.

"It's just weird," she says. "I haven't seen my room in a while."

"Well, get ready," I say, "because we're going in."

"Okay." She doesn't look ready. But it's too bad, because we don't have time to wait until she gets herself all emotionally stable. I mean, we're on a schedule here.

I open the door and step inside. It's dark, and it takes my eyes a second to adjust. Luckily, there's a tiny nightlight plugged into an outlet on the other side of the room, and that helps a little. I start walking over toward the window, figuring the balcony is the best place to start.

"Ow!" I cry as I stub my toe on something. It's a treadmill. Actually, now that I'm able to see better, it looks like Lily has a lot of exercise equipment in here. There's a weight bench in the corner, and a bunch of dumbbells resting against the wall. "I guess you like to work out," I grumble, rubbing my toe.

"No, I don't," she says, shaking her head. "This isn't . . . This stuff isn't mine."

"Really?" I ask. "You didn't have a weight bench?"

"No!" she says, sounding kind of panicked. "This isn't my room."

"We're in the wrong room?" Great. So much for her wonderful memory. Now I'm going to be lurking around up here, trying to find the right room. Probably I'll have to start opening doors. I might even accidentally end up in her mom's room. Which would be weird. I mean, no one wants to go into their parents' room. There's way too big a chance you might find something you don't want to see.

"No," Lily says, shaking her head, confused. "We're not in the wrong room."

"Yes, we are," I say, trying to keep my patience. "If this stuff isn't yours, then—"

"But I'm *sure* this is my room." She half walks, half floats over to the wall. "See?" She points to a place by the windowsill where her initials are scratched into the paint. "I carved that there when I was five."

"Okay," I say. "So then . . . *Oh.*" I nod, finally getting it. "Your parents turned your room into a gym."

"They *what*?" she screeches. "They turned my room into a *gym*? That's awful! I've only been dead for a few months!"

"Well," I say carefully, "everyone grieves in their own

way. I once helped this ghost whose parents had another baby right after she died. I mean, it wasn't like they were trying to replace her or anything. They just—"

"Whatever," Lily says. She seems like she's trying to keep herself from getting too emotional about the whole thing. "So what? They turned my bedroom into a gym. It's not like I expected them to keep everything in here the same. I'm dead, after all. It makes perfect sense."

"Okay," I say, not really certain if she means it or not. I mean, she sounds like she does, but you never can tell with ghosts. One minute they're fine; the next minute they're having a complete meltdown.

"Just because this room's a gym doesn't change what we're trying to do," she says. She has a determined look on her face, and she toys with one of the bangles on her wrist. "So let's find this balcony and get out of here."

"Okay." I cross the room to the window and look out, but there's no balcony. "It must be at the other window," I say. Which doesn't make much sense. If I remember right, that side of the house faces out onto the neighbor's property. And honestly, who wants a view of their neighbor's yard? Probably someone added it who thought they knew what they were doing. My dad has his own construction business, and he's always getting called in to help people who've messed up their houses by doing their own home improvements.

I cross the room to the other window and pull back the curtains, expecting to see a nice set of French doors. But there's nothing—just your standard window.

"There's no balcony here," I say to Lily.

"That's impossible." She crosses the room and looks outside. "But . . . I'm *positive* I fell off a balcony. And I'm positive that whatever is going to help me move on has to do with finding something in my room."

I look around and sigh. "Well, unless an exercise bike or an ab roller is essential to you moving on, I don't think we're going to find what we're looking for here."

"But we are!"

"No." I shake my head. "I've seen this happen before. See, when you die, your memories about the important stuff get all jumbled up. So you're probably not remembering everything correctly."

"But I know it was a balcony!" She's getting all insistent and raising her voice. Yikes.

"Look," I say, "I understand how you feel, but being dead, it's . . . it's different than when you were alive. I'm sure you used to have an amazing memory. But you don't realize how—"

The sound of footsteps coming up the stairs cuts me off. I freeze. Crap. I was so thrown by the fact that there was no balcony that I totally forgot about Madison.

"Come on," I whisper to Lily, and make a beeline for

the door. If I'm fast, maybe I can make it back to Madison's room before she gets there.

But just then the door to Lily's room/her parents' new gym flies open. Madison flips on the light, and blinks at me.

She takes in the scene.

Me, standing there by the elliptical. I lean against it, trying to look nonchalant.

"What are you doing in my sister's room?" she demands.

"Your sister's room?" I try to look confused. "I thought this was a gym."

"It's not." She crosses her arms over her chest. "It's my sister's room. And no one's allowed in here without my permission."

Wow. Talk about having an inflated sense of self. I mean, really. No one's allowed in her sister's room without *Madison's* permission? I doubt it.

"Oh," I say. "Sorry. I didn't know."

"Well, now you do." She looks around, like she thinks I might have made a mess or stolen something. "What were you doing in here, anyway?"

"I was, um, looking for the bathroom."

"And then you decided to walk all the way over to the window?" She raises her perfectly arched eyebrows skeptically. We definitely should have spent our makeup time on her teaching me how to get my eyebrows like that.

"Well, um, I started feeling hot." I fan myself with my hand. "And then I thought maybe I was going to faint or something. So I knew I had to get some air. So, um, I wouldn't pass out. So I was trying to get to the window."

I flutter my eyelids in what I hope is a convincing way.

Madison shakes her head. "Kendall," she says, "it is definitely time for you to leave."

"But I—"

"No." She holds her hand up like she can't take me saying another word. "Leave. Now."

Chapter

7

Well. So, obviously *that* didn't go very well.

And I can't blame anyone but myself. I mean, think about it. How stupid was I? Not listening for Madison to come back when I was snooping around in her house? Making up some ridiculous story about how I was hot and thought I might faint? Seriously, that might be the worst lie I've ever told.

I have a hard time sleeping that night. I toss and turn, my thoughts swirling around in my head like a crazy hurricane. First I think about Brandon. Then my mom. Then Madison.

I'm halfway hoping Mrs. Dunham will show up and haunt me a little, just so I'll have something else to focus on. But apparently now that me and Brandon are over, Mrs. Dunham has decided to leave me alone.

Finally, at around six o'clock, I give up and get out of bed.

I put my iPod in its speakers and turn on some music, hoping it will get me out of my funk. I crank the volume up high and let the bass shake the walls. I don't have to worry about my dad getting annoyed with me, because he left about an hour ago.

He wasn't home when I got back from Madison's last night, and so I crumpled up my note about going out so he wouldn't ask me a ton of questions. When he got home at around ten, he came upstairs and knocked on my door, but I pretended I was sleeping.

I'm still not ready to talk to him.

Since I'm awake so early, I spend the extra time doing my hair in two French braids that loop around my head. It's sort of a Princess Leia look, but a little more polished. I saw Katharine McPhee wearing her hair like this in an episode of *Smash*, and I've practiced it a couple of times on the weekend, but I never had time to do it on a weekday until now.

Once I'm done with my hair, I pull a long white V-neck sweater on over my fave black skinny jeans, and then tuck the bottom of my pants into my boots. They're not as cute as Madison's, obviously, but they're still pretty cute. And they're cozy.

Then I grab the scarf she gave me off the hook on the back of my door and loop it around my neck. Hopefully, when she sees me wearing her scarf, she'll remember that we're supposed to be friends. I'm going to have to get back on her good side somehow, and maybe this will be a good start.

"That scarf is a good touch," Lily says, nodding in approval as we walk to the bus stop.

"Thanks."

Lily's been quiet this morning, sitting on my bed most of the time, looking out the window and not really moving except to drum her fingers to my music. Which is fine with me. I'm not really in the mood to talk.

On the ride to school I listen to my iPod and stare out the window, zoning out as I watch the houses zoom by.

I walk into school with my music still on. I'm at my locker, getting my books for the morning, when someone yanks the earbud out of my ear.

I shriek and turn around, expecting to see Mr. Jacobi or another teacher standing there. We're not supposed to be wearing our iPods in school, but since school hasn't *technically* started yet, I figured I could get away with it. But it's not Mr. Jacobi standing there. And it's not another teacher. It's Ellie.

I'm so shocked and happy to see her that for a moment I can't find my voice.

"Hi," I say finally.

She doesn't reply. She just stands there, looking at me. I know it has only been a couple of days, but I miss her so much, it hurts. I'm used to talking to her multiple times a day, every day. Not being able to just call her or text her whenever I want has been torture.

The way she's looking at me is making me a little nervous, though. Why isn't she saying anything? Obviously, she wants to talk, right? Or else she wouldn't have come over here and pulled my earbud out of my ear.

"What's up?" I try. I pull some of my books out of my bag and slide them into my locker.

"Anything you want to tell me?" She sounds mad.

"Um, what do you mean?" I'm not trying to stall or be smart. There are a million things Ellie could be talking about. Like me seeing ghosts, me lying to my dad about going to see my mom, me—

"Oh, I don't know," she says, all sarcastic-like. Jasmine Flavia, who has the locker next to mine, is trying to put her books away, so Ellie moves to my other side. The only problem with that is, now my locker door is in between us. Ellie solves that problem by reaching out and slamming it shut.

"Hey!" I say. "I wasn't done."

"Maybe your new friend Madison can help you," Ellie says. "Now that you two are besties. Or should I say ex-besties?"

I'm having trouble keeping up with this conversation. "I'm having trouble keeping up with this conversation," I say. I reach out and start twirling my lock so I can open my locker again, but then I decide I probably shouldn't do that if Ellie wants to talk. If there's any chance we can make up, I should be giving her my undivided attention.

"So why didn't you tell me?" she asks, her eyes accusing.

Again, there's a million things she could be talking about. "Why didn't I tell you what?"

"About you and Madison Baker!" She says "Madison Baker" like it's equivalent to the devil. Which it kind of is.

"I don't think this girl likes my sister," Lily says, sighing. She doesn't say it in an accusing way, though. She says it more like she's used to people not liking her sister, and she's bored of it. She turns around and wanders off down the hallway.

I'm glad Lily's not the kind of ghost I have to worry about. The last two I had to help? Forget it. I couldn't let them out of my sight for a second.

"Me and Madison Baker? What about us?"

Ellie's eyes look like they're going to bug out of her head. "How you went over to her house last night!"

"Oh." I turn back to my locker and start to twirl the combination lock again, mostly because I need something to keep my hands busy while I figure out what to say. "I didn't know you cared."

"Of course I care!" Ellie says. "You're my best friend."

"Well, how was I supposed to know that?" I ask softly. I slide my locker door open so she can't see my face, because I'm pretty sure I'm going to start crying. "I thought you never wanted to talk to me again."

Ellie reaches out and shuts my locker halfway so she can see me. "I never said that."

"You didn't really have to *say* it. I mean, you brought all my stuff over to my house and dumped it on my front porch."

She sighs, and I can see the mental battle going on inside her. "I don't hate you, Kendall," she says finally. "I'm just mad. And confused."

"Ellie, I didn't mean to hurt you," I say. "And I definitely didn't mean to lie to you."

"Then why did you?"

Good question. "I don't know." It's not a truthful answer, obviously. I might lose Ellie anyway, but if I tell her about the ghosts, then I'll definitely lose her. I take a deep breath. "It's complicated. But I didn't do it just to lie to you." I slide my locker door open and finish gathering the books I need for my morning classes. I try to think if there's something I can say that might not technically be a lie, but I can't come up with anything. "Look," I say finally, "Micah was upset about his sister who died, and I was helping him."

Ellie shakes her head. "I don't believe you."

I don't say anything.

"I don't understand," she says. "If you like Micah and you don't like Brandon, then why didn't you just tell me?"

"I don't like Micah."

"Yeah, well, that's not what Madison Baker is telling everyone." She shifts her book bag on her shoulder and bites her lip. "And honestly, Kendall, that's not the only thing she's saying."

"What do you mean?" I ask, a sick feeling rising in my throat.

The bell rings then, and Ellie looks over her shoulder down the hall. "We should get to homeroom."

But neither of us moves.

"We could go talk . . . ," I offer, holding my breath.

"You mean skip?"

I nod. Ellie and I just skipped a class a few days ago, when I started having a meltdown about Brandon. It was the first time I ever skipped a class, and now here I am a few days later, suggesting we do it again. Apparently, I've gone rogue.

She leans in. "I don't know," she says. "Last time we skipped, we ended up under the stairwell, and that was weird." She shakes her head. "So many people walking up and down."

I swallow. "We could leave school and then come back.

We could pretend we were just late or something."

"Don't you need a note to be late?"

"I'm not sure."

She thinks about it, then looks over her shoulder at the rush of kids all taking off toward their homerooms. She takes a step toward them, and I'm sure she's going to say no and head to homeroom.

But then she turns around, and her eyes soften, and I catch a glimpse of the Ellie who's my best friend, the Ellie who took care of me last year when I had the flu, the Ellie who always compliments me on my crazy hairstyles, the Ellie who would do anything for me.

"Okay," she says, her face breaking into a smile. "Let's do it."

The key to doing something wrong and not getting caught is looking confident. So when Ellie and I walk out of school, I make sure to keep my shoulders back and my head held high.

Ellie, however, apparently doesn't know this rule. Which makes sense. I mean, I have a lot more experience when it comes to doing things I'm not supposed to. (See: taking off to see my mom, lurking around Madison Baker's house, etc., etc.)

Ellie scuttles along, her head down, keeping her eyes on the sidewalk except for when she looks up to take furtive glances over her shoulder to make sure no one's behind us.

"Where are we going?" she whispers to me.

Good question. "Um, the coffee shop on the corner?"

There's a coffee shop right across from school. I've never been there, but my bus always passes it.

"Isn't that a little too close?" Ellie asks. "What if we see someone from school?"

"Everyone from school is in homeroom," I point out.

"Oh." She nods. "Good point."

The coffee shop is warm and inviting, and the delicious smell of cinnamon and coffee hits my nose as soon as we get inside.

Suddenly I'm ravenous.

"I didn't have breakfast," I tell Ellie. "I'm going to get a cinnamon bun. You want anything?"

"Just a coffee."

Ellie gets us a table while I stand in line to get the food and drinks. The coffee shop is busy, mostly with people grabbing their morning joe before heading off to work.

I concoct a whole story in my head about how I'm homeschooled, just in case the people working here ask why I'm not in school, but when it's my turn, the cashier, an older woman with a purple streak in her black hair, takes my money and hands me my change without saying a word.

When I get back to the table, Ellie's looking out the window, a sad look on her face.

"Here you go," I say, setting her coffee down in front of her. "I, um, put cream and sugar in it for you. And I know you said you weren't hungry, but I got you this chocolate chip cookie because it looked good."

"Thanks." Her hands wrap around the oversize white mug, and she stares at the cookie blankly.

I sit down across from her, not sure how things can be so awkward with someone I was so close to up until a few days ago.

I look outside to where a few snowflakes are starting to fall.

"It's snowing!" I say happily.

"Great," she grumbles. "Now we're in for months of cold weather and dirty, slushy sidewalks."

Wow. Way to be pessimistic.

"So what is Madison Baker saying about me?" I ask. Maybe sharing gossip about me will cheer Ellie up, since she's apparently harboring some latent hostility.

But I'm wrong, because Ellie shifts on her chair. "What do you mean?"

"You said Madison was saying things about me." I rip off a piece of warm, gooey cinnamon bun and pop it into my mouth. Yum. I'm going to have a huge sugar crash after this, but I don't even care. It's so worth it.

"Madison Baker loves to gossip," Ellie says, waving her hand like whatever Madison is saying is totally inconsequential. "You shouldn't even worry about it."

"Oh, I'm not *worried* about it," I lie. Let's face it, no one wants one of the most popular girls in school gossiping about them. Gossiping on any level is not okay, but having Madison do it is the worst.

"Good," Ellie says. "Because you have enough to worry about."

I nod. I don't know what she's talking about, that I have enough to worry about. Does she think I'm crazy?

"So what is she saying, though?" I ask nonchalantly. "Just so we can, you know, laugh about it."

Ellie reaches over and grabs a piece of my cinnamon bun, which makes me ridiculously happy. She wouldn't be sharing food with me if she was that mad, would she?

"Just dumb stuff." She takes a deep breath. "About how you came over to her house and started snooping around in her dead sister's room."

"I wasn't snooping around!" I protest. "I was looking for the bathroom! I *told* her that."

"Yeah." Ellie shrugs like it doesn't matter, then finishes chewing her cinnamon bun. "Kendall, what's going on with you?"

"What do you mean?"

"I just . . . I *miss* you. And I don't know why you lied to me about Micah, or why you're hanging out with Madison." She frowns. "And it's really frustrating, because you and I have never kept secrets from each other."

"That's not true," I point out. "When you got me those Taylor Swift tickets for my birthday last year, it was a total surprise." I smile, but Ellie doesn't smile back.

She looks out the window and doesn't say anything for a moment. "The thing is, if you're having a hard time, I want to be there for you. But I'm also angry at you, Kendall. I really am."

"I know," I say. "But you have to believe me when I say I don't like Micah. I really was just being a friend, talking to him about his sister."

"Then why didn't you just *tell* me that?"

Good question. "Because he asked me not to say anything. He didn't want anyone to know he was hurting. You know, because he was new here. He didn't want people to think he was a freak." Lie, lie, lie.

She nods. "I guess that makes sense. But then why were you hanging out with Madison?"

I take a deep breath. "I just felt so alone," I say. "No one was talking to me, and I guess I kind of freaked out. I mean, you and Kyle and Brandon had totally turned your backs on me. And so when Madison asked me over, I said yes. I guess I was in a vulnerable state."

She wrinkles her nose. "But Madison *Baker*?"

"I know, she's awful." I wonder what Ellie's going to think when I still have to try to become friends with Madison. Oh, well. I'll cross that bridge when I come to it. "I can't believe she's telling people I was snooping around her house!"

"In her sister's old room," Ellie adds.

"Which isn't even her sister's room anymore," I say. "It's a gym now."

"Oh," Ellie says. "Then why is she freaking out so much?"

"I don't know. Because she's Madison Baker?"

Ellie laughs. "Yeah, probably. I wonder if her parents turned that room into a gym when Lily died, or when she went away to college."

I almost choke on my cinnamon bun. "Madison's sister was away at college?" How did I not know about this? I really need to start paying more attention to the details of people's deaths. It's my professional responsibility.

"Yeah," Ellie says. "She was going to be a freshman at Sadler State, but she'd already started some summer program there when she died. I know because I ran into Madison at the mall last year, and she was bragging about how her sister was going to take her to parties where Madison was going to flirt with college boys. As if!"

Ellie starts going on and on about how much of a liar Madison is, but I'm kind of tuning out. All I can think about is that Lily was at *college*. And that means she might have gotten confused, and whatever it is that's keeping her from moving on might be in the room she had there.

Lily probably wasn't talking about her *bed*room—she was talking about her dorm room. And if she *is* talking about her dorm room, obviously I'll have to find a way to get into it. But on the bright side, I won't have to put up with Madison Baker anymore. I'm free, free, free!

I'm so happy and giddy that when I hear the voice, I don't register who it is.

"Is this chair taken?" it asks, all snotty-like.

I don't look up at the rude talker, just push the empty chair that's sitting at our table a few inches toward him. "Nope," I say. "It's all yours."

"Good," the person says.

And that's when I realize why the voice sounds familiar.

I look up, and my heart slides up to my throat, then down through my stomach and out my shoes.

"Kendall Williams," Mr. Jacobi says. "Fancy seeing you here. Do you want to explain to me why you're not in first period?"

Chapter 8

Mr. Jacobi marches me and Ellie right back to school and to the main office, where we get written up not only for skipping class but for leaving campus to do it. Apparently, skipping school and staying on school grounds isn't as bad as if you leave. I guess it's some kind of liability issue or something.

The principal calls my dad, but luckily my dad doesn't ask to talk to me. He just thanks them for letting him know and says he'll deal with me when I get home. Hopefully, he'll understand I'm in a weakened emotional state and cut me some slack.

Ellie's parents are pretty chill about it too, at least at first, but still. I feel horrible for getting her in trouble. I mean, let's face it, she wouldn't even have *been* skipping if it weren't for me.

When the principal is done calling our parents, he makes us go to class.

The day passes at a snail's pace.

Madison has apparently decided I'm crazy, so every time I see her in the hall, she whispers about me to whoever is next to her and then giggles and turns her back.

At lunch things are super-awkward. Even though Ellie and I have made up, obviously I can't sit at my normal lunch table. *Brandon's* at that lunch table. So I pick a different table, and then Ellie moves over to sit with me, and then I start having tons of guilt, because if it wasn't for me, Ellie would be sitting at her usual table with Kyle. But instead she's having to give up what she wants, for a best friend who's lying to her.

It's so awful.

To make matters worse, after school is our first official tutoring session at Stoneridge Elementary School.

And since I have no one to talk to as we walk over, I end up at the back of the line, talking to Lily.

"So get this," I say, making sure to keep my voice low so no one else can hear me. "Apparently, you were in college. At a summer program, and then you were going to be a freshman."

She frowns. "Really? That's so cool. Leave it to me to

end up dying while I'm in college. I mean, all I ever wanted to do was get out of high school, and just when I get my chance, I die."

I roll my eyes. "Right, like you really wanted to get out of high school."

"Of course I did," she says. "High school was horrible."

"Riiigght." Lily's gorgeous. I highly doubt she had to worry about the normal high school problems, like mean girls or boys not liking her back.

"Why are you looking at me like that?" she asks as she flicks a perfectly curled glossy tendril of hair over her shoulder. I wonder how she gets her hair to stay so perfect. Maybe it's a ghost thing. If you can't be affected by things like wind and rain, it's probably hard for your hair to get messed up.

"I don't know," I say slowly. "It's just that you seem so . . . ah, put together."

"Things aren't always as they seem, Kendall."

I nod. "Tell me about it."

She takes in a deep breath and then blows it out. "So I'm in college?"

"Yeah, at Sadler State."

"Oh, fun!" She brightens. "I always wanted to go there."

"Good for you," I say, halfway meaning it. "Anyway, that explains why you didn't have a balcony in your room at home." The snow that started while I was in the coffee shop with Ellie never really stopped, and little flakes are falling all around us, joining the dusting that's already on the ground. I turn my face up toward the sky, letting a flake fall on my nose. My face is warm for some reason, and the cold flakes feel good.

"I don't get it," Lily says, frowning.

"Well, you said whatever it is you're moving on from had to do with your room. And you also said you fell off a balcony. But your bedroom at home didn't *have* a balcony, and since your parents turned it into an exercise room, I really doubt whatever it is you're looking for is still there. So it must be in your room at school."

She claps her hands excitedly. "So now all we have to do is go to my room at school!"

Wow. She makes it sound so simple. Poor, naïve little Lily. "Yup," I say. "Except I'll have to figure out a way to get into the room, so that could be a problem."

She shrugs, like me getting into her room is a difficulty that's totally inconsequential to her. Which I guess in a way it is. I mean, there's nothing she can really do to help me. I'm going to have to figure it out on my own.

I sigh.

How can I get into Lily's room? I wonder if she had a roommate. Probably. Maybe I can figure out a way to get close to her roommate, and then come up with some kind of excuse for why I have to get into the room.

Of course, first I'm going to have to figure out a way to actually get to Sadler State. I don't think it's too far from here, but I'm definitely going to need a ride. And I really doubt my dad is going to drive me, not after what—

"Hi," a voice next to me says.

"Hi," I answer back automatically, not really paying attention to who it is. But when I turn, I have to bite back a groan. Madison.

"How's it going?" she asks, all happy, like we're old friends and not at all like she spent all day telling the whole school that I'm crazy and went snooping around her house.

"Fine." I shrug, not really wanting to get into some big discussion with her. I don't want to antagonize her either, though, so I guess I have to at least be a little bit nice to her. "How are you?"

"Fine." She sighs. "I just wanted to ask you if you're okay with me and Brandon going on a date."

I feel bile rise into my throat. Brandon asked Madison out on a date? I look toward the front of the group, where I can see Brandon's head bobbing through the crowd. I know Madison's pretty and everything, and I know she's been after him pretty hard-core, but I guess a part of me always held out hope that Brandon would be smart enough to stay away from her.

I struggle to retain my composure. "Oh. Um, you don't have to ask me that. You know that I like Micah now."

"Who's Micah?" Lily asks. "Is he the one you were talking to yesterday? He's kind of weird. I saw him throw his empty water bottle onto the floor in the hallway when he thought no one was looking."

"Great!" Madison says, beaming at me like I just gave her the best news in the whole world. "So then it's all settled."

"Yup!" I beam back at her. I expect her to start chattering away about her and Brandon, but she doesn't. She starts to walk back toward the front of the group. Which I guess makes sense. She probably wants to walk with Brandon. *I will not cry, I will not cry, I will not cry.* I wish Ellie were here. If I have to see Brandon and Madison holding hands, I'm going to freak out.

"Oh!" Madison says, turning back around. "Just one more thing. I need my scarf back." She holds her hand out expectantly.

"You need your scarf back?" My hands fly to my neck and finger the silky material. "But you gave it to me."

She looks at me like I'm crazy. "No, I didn't. You asked if you could borrow it, and I said yes."

My eyes are about to bug out of my head. That is so not what happened. What happened was that Madison gave me the scarf. I didn't even ask her if I could borrow it, much less have it.

But she's still holding out her hand.

And I'm not sure why, but it's like something inside me snaps. I'm sick of Madison Baker. Sick of being scared of her, sick of always wondering and worrying about her talking to Brandon or talking about me. And when I think about it, I realize she has no power over me anymore.

If she's really going to start dating Brandon, then I don't have anything to freak out about. It's over. They're together. And if I need to go to Sadler State to help Lily, then there's nothing Madison can do for me at this point anyway.

The thought is strangely freeing.

"No," I say. It feels like I'm talking loudly, but it must come out in a whisper, because Madison shows no sign of hearing me.

"Give it back," she repeats, sounding annoyed this time. She's facing me, walking backward as she goes. I know it's mean to think this, but it wouldn't be the worst thing in the world if she fell. Not that I want her to get seriously hurt or anything. But a skinned knee and a few moments of embarrassment wouldn't be the end of the world.

"No," I say, louder this time.

Lily gasps.

Madison gasps.

Actually, they both gasp at the same time, which is kind of funny. Since they're sisters, they have similar tones in their voices, and so it's like a gasp in stereo.

I laugh.

Which just makes Madison angrier.

"What did you say?" she asks.

"I said no." I shrug. "You gave me this scarf. So you can't take it back now. It's, like, illegal." It's totally true, too. I saw it on an episode of *Judge Judy*, where this woman gave her shady ex-boyfriend a bunch of money because he claimed he was broke and couldn't pay his rent. And then she found out he'd spent the money on a new stereo system, so she was all, "Judge Judy, Judge Judy, that money wasn't given to him. He just borrowed it, and now he better give it back."

And Judge Judy totally laughed her out of the courtroom.

Not that me and Madison are going to end up on *Judge Judy*. We're minors. And I don't think Judge Judy likes kids in her courtroom unless it's absolutely necessary.

"I didn't *give* it to you," Madison says. "I let you borrow it. Now give it back."

"No, thanks," I say.

She narrows her eyes at me, and for a second I think she's going to go completely postal. But then she flips her hair over her shoulder and shakes her head. "Wow," she says. "You really are crazy. I mean, all this time I was *telling* people you were crazy, but I was mostly doing it just to have something to gossip about. But you really are nuts."

"Oh, Madison," I say, smiling. "You have no idea."

Lily laughs at this, which makes me happy. I mean, if Lily's laughing at a joke at her sister's expense, then it has to be pretty funny. It's also true. If Madison knew I could see ghosts, she would truly think I was off my rocker.

The whole thing is hilarious when you think about it.

It's so hilarious that I start to laugh.

"What's so funny?" Madison demands.

"Private joke," I say. Which makes me laugh even harder.

Madison doesn't like this. She walks back toward me and tugs at the bottom of my scarf. "Give it back," she says. "I'm serious."

"No, *I'm* serious," I say, turning away from her.

I quicken my pace because we're at the bottom of the long circular driveway that leads up to the elementary school now. Wow. I never realized how much of a steep hill this driveway's on. Leave it to me to end up having to get away from the most popular girl in school on an incline.

As I try to pass by her, Madison reaches out and grabs the scarf.

"Stop," I say, trying to shake her off. But she pulls harder, and I turn my body around in an effort to keep from getting choked. It works—I don't get choked, but the scarf comes off my neck, and Madison is somehow able to keep hold of it.

I grab the other end and hold tight.

She pulls hard.

I pull harder.

She yanks it with such force that I have to take a few big steps toward her to keep my footing.

Then I tug it back so she has to come toward me.

"Give it up, Baker," I say. Wow. I've never called someone by their last name before. It sounds kind of gangster. I think I like it. "You gave me this scarf, Baker," I say, trying it out again.

"Stop calling me 'Baker,'" she says, pulling the silky fabric back toward her. "And let go of the scarf!"

"No!"

"Yes!"

"No!"

This whole time we've somehow been able to keep walking toward the elementary school. Who knew that fighting over a scarf could be so conducive to multitasking?

"LET GO OF THE SCARF!" Madison yells so loudly that a couple of people turn to look.

"No!" I yell back. "You gave it to me."

"This is getting out of hand," Lily says, sounding worried. Her beautiful violet eyes are wide. She should probably fade away, the way ghosts sometimes do when they get overwhelmed. She's definitely too innocent to be seeing this kind of thing. "And you guys better stop before—"

RRRRRIIIP.

The scarf tears down the middle, leaving me and Madison each holding a piece of the silky, shimmery, beautiful fabric.

"Oh my God," I say. What a waste. That scarf had to be expensive, and now it's wrecked. I look down at the piece in my hand, wondering if there's any possible way it can be sewn back together. But I doubt it. I'm sure the fabric is way too delicate for that.

"Look what you did!" Madison shrieks. Her face is all red, and she looks super-mad. Madder than the time she and Katie Dobbs wore the same dress to school, even.

"I didn't do it," I say. "You did." I'm still holding my piece of the scarf, and I get a secret thrill of satisfaction when I see it's the bigger piece. If someone had to decide whose ripped scarf this was, they would definitely have to rule that it belonged to me. Possession is nine tenths of the law, or whatever it is they say.

Madison's eyes start to bug out of her head even more, and her face turns even redder. I don't know why she's getting so worked up about a dumb scarf. I mean, she stole Brandon from me. Isn't that enough for her? Apparently not, because the next thing I know, Madison starts to take a few steps toward me.

"You're dead, Williams," she says.

Okay, now I'm kind of scared. I don't want to *fight* Madison. It's one thing to talk crap to her and call her by her last name, but—

"Girls!" Mr. Jacobi appears between us, breaking it up. And that's when I realize that the rest of our classmates have formed a loose circle around us, watching the drama unfold. "This is very unbecoming behavior, especially when we are guests at another school, one in which we are supposed to be setting examples for impressionable young minds!" He shakes his head in disgust, like he can't believe what hooligans we are. "I thought you would know better than this." He turns his attention toward me. "Especially you, Kendall. I would certainly think you'd want to be on your best behavior after what happened earlier."

"Yes, Mr. Jacobi," I say. Trying to explain would be pointless. Especially since it's not like I'm completely innocent in the whole thing.

"Now, are you girls done with this little display of immature behavior, or do we have to go back to school and have your parents come pick you up early?"

"No," Madison says quickly. "We're done with it."

"Good choice," Lily says. "My parents would totally freak out if they found out Madison almost got into a fistfight."

"Good," Mr. Jacobi says. "Now please come inside. And I trust this will be the last I'll hear out of you two for the rest of the afternoon."

We all start to traipse toward the double doors of the school. Right when we're about to go in, I catch Brandon looking at me. My heart does a weird fluttery thing. What does he think about me and Madison fighting? Does he think it had to do with him asking her out? Does he think I'm even crazier than he already thought? Is he going to get a restraining order against me?

I open my mouth to say something to reassure him, something brilliant like *That wasn't about you; it was about a scarf*, but I chicken out.

And then he passes through the revolving doors and into the elementary school, leaving me standing there in the snow.

Chapter 9

Mr. Jacobi hustles us into the library of the elementary school, which is so cheery, I can't stand it. There are life-size pictures of fictional characters on the walls, like Nancy Drew and Encyclopedia Brown and Harry Potter and Percy Jackson. There's a display set up on a table in the middle of the room with a bunch of books and a big poster board that says, READ THESE BOOKS BY OUR STUDENT AUTHORS!

Which is crazy. I mean, I've thought about being a writer for as long as I can remember, and the most I've ever written are lists of information that ghosts tell me. And these kids, who are way younger than me, are writing *books*. I'm sure they're short books, but still. A book is a book.

Hmm. Maybe my ghost notebook will turn out to be helpful someday. Maybe I'll end up writing a book about all my adventures. Starring a girl my age who can see ghosts and ends up having to break up with her boyfriend because of it. They always say to write what you know, and that's a story I know quite a lot about.

"Welcome," Mr. Jacobi says when we're all gathered around him, standing in between the tables. "Now, as you know, the peer tutoring program is new this year, and so we're all kind of flying blind here." He chuckles to himself, but no one else laughs.

"What we're going to do is break you up into new groups. We decided it would be best to have groups of four and have a mix of seventh and eighth graders in each group. That way, if your students are having problems with a particular skill set, there will most likely be a middle school student in your group who can help."

We're going to be getting new groups! That's the best news I've heard all day. Could you imagine being stuck with Brandon and Madison? Shudder. Especially after what just happened between us outside. Madison might try to maul me or something.

"Hey!" a voice chirps next to my ear. Oh. Micah.

I don't answer, just give him a tight smile and hope he gets the message. Which is that he should go away and leave me alone. But he doesn't.

Instead, he moves closer. "So you've been kind of mysterious lately," he says. "You haven't been to the salon. And we never really got a chance to talk about how you ran out of the bowling alley the other night." He raises his eyebrows at me and gives me a smirk, like he's waiting for me to let him in on some kind of secret.

Leave it to Micah to think I'm being mysterious. Did it ever maybe cross his mind that something's wrong? That I didn't run out of the bowling alley or avoid him as some kind of ploy to get him to like me more, but that I might have actually been upset about something?

"Yeah, well, it was kind of weird when my boyfriend caught me there with you," I say.

Micah laughs. "So Brandon was mad?"

"You could say that."

"You guys weren't meant to be, anyway." He grins. "Otherwise you wouldn't have been hanging out with me, babe."

"Don't call me 'babe.' And we weren't really hanging out."

"Does everyone have a group?" Mr. Jacobi calls. I look around. During the time I was having this very interesting (not) conversation with Micah, apparently everyone else was choosing their groups. Great.

I look around quickly to see if anyone needs a fourth person. There's nothing worse than not having a group. If you don't have a group, the teacher has to assign you to one, and that pretty much lets everyone else know you're a loser. And why is Mr. Jacobi trusting us to pick our own groups, anyway? Kids are horrible at that, especially if we're supposed to make sure we have a mix of seventh and eighth graders in each one.

I'm just about to raise my hand and let Mr. Jacobi know I'm stranded (which he's probably going to be super-happy about because, let's face it, he hates me), but Micah beats me to it.

"Me and Kendall are partners," he announces. "So we need two more people."

Wow. Talk about being presumptuous. Although this is one time I'm actually happy Micah is acting like we're together. At least now it looks like I have someone who wants to work with me.

"Anyone else?" Mr. Jacobi asks us, annoyed. His eyes slip around the room. "Does anyone else not have a full group?"

No one says anything. Although it's kind of hard to hear Mr. Jacobi. He's talking pretty loudly, but the class is being louder. They're all excited at the prospect of being in groups.

I look around the room, hoping that someone else is going to need a group. The last thing I want is for me and Micah to be stuck working together alone. How totally awkward.

"Who doesn't have a group?" Mr. Jacobi screeches. "The amount of students here is equally divisible by four! Everyone should be in groups of four. That is why I chose four as a number!" Wow, he's really bent out of shape about this whole four-people-in-a-group thing. I wonder if maybe Mr. Jacobi has OCD. I saw a show about that on TLC. People who have it need to make sure everything is in multiples of the perfect number, and they get really anxious if it doesn't happen. It would definitely explain a lot about his mental state.

"We don't have a full group," a boy's voice says. Oh, thank God. Now I won't have to be stuck all alone with Micah. Although I really hope it's not Jason Fields we end up with. That kid's the worst.

"Who?" Mr. Jacobi demands. "Who is that talking?" He stands up on his tiptoes and looks over the crowd, trying to see who it is who's raising their hand.

I look too. And when I see who it is, my heart stops. It's Brandon. And Madison. Brandon and Madison are going to be the other two people in our group.

"Good," Mr. Jacobi says. "Brandon Dunham and Madison Baker, please join Kendall and Micah. I realize that you are all in the same grade, but I see we're short eighth graders."

My hand immediately shoots into the air. "Mr. Jacobi," I say, "I really don't think it's the best idea for me and Madison to be working together." He gives me a blank stare, like he has completely forgotten that me and Madison were just about to tear each other's throats out. "You know, because of the, uh . . . because of what just happened outside."

Mr. Jacobi pulls himself up to his full height (which can't be more than five and a half feet) and says, "Ms. Williams, are you saying that you're unable to work with Ms. Baker?"

"Yes, that's exactly what I'm saying." Is Mr. Jacobi crazy? Maybe memory loss is one of the complications of his OCD. Although it definitely didn't mention anything about that in the show I saw.

"So if you are unable to exist in a group situation, does that mean you are unable to complete this extra credit?"

"No," I say, frustrated. "That's not what I'm saying. I'm saying I should probably have another group. Or that maybe me and Micah should just work alone."

Next to me, Micah smirks. But I'm past the point of caring. Even working by myself with Micah is preferable to working with Madison and Brandon. That's a disaster waiting to happen, not to mention the mental stress it would bestow upon me.

"So you're saying you should get special treatment?" Mr. Jacobi laughs. "Everyone else here is able to work in a group of four. But if you don't think you're able to play by the rules, Ms. Williams, then you're free to wait in the main office until we're finished, and then I will remove you from the program."

He gives me a stern look, and I know he's thinking about the fact that if I don't get this extra credit, I'm probably going to fail math.

"No, that's okay," I mumble.

"Good," he says.

"Don't worry, babe," Micah says, slinging his arm over my shoulder. "We're going to have a great time."

Yeah. Really great.

"Everyone chose a table to sit at, and then we will bring in the students!" Mr. Jacobi says with a flourish, like he's the emcee at a Justin Bieber concert and not just announcing that some little kids are coming into the library to meet with us.

Everyone starts choosing their tables.

Madison and Brandon sit down at a table on the other side of the room. Of course. Leave it to Madison to just expect us to go over to where she's sitting, instead of picking a table in the middle of the room. Ugh. How annoying.

Micah and I make our way over to their table.

"What's up, Micah?" Madison purrs. She stands up and reaches out to hug him. Which makes no sense. Why would she be hugging Micah? I thought her and Brandon were a thing now. Then I realize she's doing it because she thinks *I* like Micah. So of course she would make it a point to go out of her way to flirt with him. Ugh.

"Not much," Micah says, hugging her right back. So much for loyalty. "What's up with you?"

"You know, the usual." She sighs and gives a little giggle, like her life is so crazy and exciting, she can't even explain everything that's going on.

I sit down across from Madison, mostly because I don't want to be sitting across from Brandon. Actually, I don't even want to *look* at Brandon. I wonder if I can get away with doing this whole entire tutoring session without looking at him once.

Not looking, not looking, not looking.

I wonder how long I can go. Five seconds . . . ten seconds . . . Wow, this is easier than I thought. What would be the point of looking at him, anyway? Just so I can see how totally adorable he is? Thirty seconds, forty seconds . . . one minute.

One minute without looking! Wow, I am so over him, it's crazy. Why didn't I realize how over him I was?

I have a little cheering party in my head for myself.

And then sneak a glance at Brandon.

Oops.

He's wearing a soft-looking yellow fleece over a hunter-green T-shirt that brings out his eyes. I never appreciated his eyes as much as I should have when we were together. And then I catch Madison catching *me* looking at Brandon. She gives me a little smirk.

Brandon has his head down, and he's looking through the papers in his binder. Which I'm sure is just a distraction technique. There's no way he's really that concerned with whatever's in his math binder.

"So," Micah says. "How much work do you think we're really going to have to do today?"

"I don't know," Madison says. She wrinkles up her nose. "Hopefully, we'll get some kids that are already halfway smart."

"I don't think that's the point," Brandon says. "It's the kids who are having trouble who need to stay after and get help. Not the smart ones."

"Well, maybe we'll get lucky," Micah says. He rolls an old homework paper into a ball and starts pushing it around on the table. "Kendall," he says. "Go long!"

He bats the paper at me, but I'm so taken off guard that it just flies by and onto the floor.

"Oh," I say, "sorry. I wasn't expecting that."

"It's okay." Micah gets up and picks the paper up off the floor, then starts bouncing it up and down on his hand like a volleyball. Madison giggles, like it's the funniest thing she's ever seen.

I open up to a fresh page in my notebook, then pick up my pencil, but there's really nothing for me to write. Where are the kids, anyway? Shouldn't they be here already?

Micah sits down and keeps playing with his homemade ball.

Bounce.

Bounce.

Crinkle.

Bounce.

Micah keeps bouncing, until the paper bounces off his hand and hits me in the head.

"Ow!" I say automatically. It's not that it really hurt that much. It was just kind of annoying.

"Sorry." Micah shrugs and gets up to retrieve the paper from the floor.

Madison laughs. "That was hilarious."

"You should be more careful," Brandon says to Micah. He turns to me. "You okay?"

"Yeah," I manage. "I'm fine."

"You have a cut on your forehead," Madison points out helpfully, then wrinkles her nose in distaste.

"I do?" My hand flies to my forehead, and I'm half expecting to come away with a handful of blood. But there's nothing.

"It's not a cut," Brandon says, giving Madison a dirty look. He turns back to me. "It's just a scratch. You can't even really see it."

"Thanks," I say.

He looks at me and his face softens, like maybe he's going to say something else. But then he just nods and turns his attention back to Micah. "You need to stop doing that," he says. "We're supposed to be setting a good example for the kids."

Micah gives him a cocky grin and then bounces the paper again. Brandon reaches out, grabs the ball out of the air, and then throws it into the garbage. Wow. Things are getting tense around here.

Micah stares at him, like he can't believe Brandon just did that. *I* can't really believe Brandon just did that. It was so . . . *manly*. Was Brandon sticking up for me? And if so, does that mean he might still like me?

And then, like some kind of sign from God, I spot Mrs. Dunham lurking over by a shelf of biographies.

"Oh my God!" I say giddily. I've never been so happy to see her in my life. Mrs. Dunham wouldn't be here if she didn't want to keep an eye on me. And the only reason she has ever wanted to keep an eye on me is so she can make sure I stay away from Brandon. Does that mean Brandon and I have a chance? Does that mean he still might like me a little? He wouldn't have yelled at Micah if he didn't still like me a little, right?

"What?" Madison asks.

"Nothing," I say.

"God, you are so weird." She shakes her head and rolls her eyes, then grabs a strand of her hair and starts looking for split ends.

"Give me back my paper ball," Micah demands. He

reaches across the table, like he's waiting for Brandon to put it back in his hand. Which is ridiculous, since Brandon threw it into the garbage. He can't give it back.

"No," Brandon says.He rolls his eyes, like Micah is acting crazy. Which he is.

"You better get me that paper back, or I'm going to—"

But the rest of Micah's threat is cut off by the sound of a million screaming voices entering the library. The children have arrived.

So it turns out it wasn't a million children. It was more like twenty-five of them. I had no idea twenty-five children could make that much noise, but they can. Anyway, twenty-five children seems like a lot to me, but apparently it's not what Mr. Jacobi was hoping for.

"This isn't what was supposed to happen," he says, looking down at his paper in dismay. "We were supposed to have more children."

He's all freaked out because now each group is going to have to share a single child, instead of each of us getting assigned our own.

Which is actually better. Because this way it will be a lot less work."Hello," our kid says as she sits down at our table. She has blond hair and cornflower-blue eyes, and her hair is pulled back into two beautiful pigtails that have the perfect amount of curl at the bottom. Her skin is clean and shiny.

I look around at the rest of the library. Children are running around and causing all kinds of chaos. At the table next to us, a boy grabs a stuffed dog off one of the library shelves and starts to pretend it's peeing on chair legs. Yikes.

I turn back to the little girl sitting next to me. She crosses her legs and folds her hands on the table in front of her, all prim and proper. I breathe a sigh of relief that we got her and not one of those hooligans.

"What's your name, sweetie?" I ask.

"Vivienne."

"What a beautiful name."

"Thank you very much." This girl is an angel! I am definitely going to be her favorite tutor, I can already tell. I'll be like the older sister she never had. No way she's going to be bonding with Madison. In fact, Madison already looks bored. She has pulled a magazine out of her backpack and is flipping through the pages. Talk about not wanting to make a lasting impression on the youth of today.

"So what is it you need help with, Vivienne?" Brandon asks her nicely.

Micah isn't even looking at Vivienne. He has taken another piece of paper and turned it into a new bouncing ball. Every few seconds he takes his eye off his bouncing and looks over at Brandon, like he's waiting for a reaction from him. But Brandon's not biting.

"I don't really need any help," Vivienne says.

How cute! She's, like, afraid we're going to be inconvenienced by helping her.

"It's okay, honey," I tell her. "That's what we're here for."

She sighs and sort of scrunches up her lips. Then her eyes fall on Madison's magazine. "Is that the new *SMOOCH*?" she asks.

"Yeah," Madison says without looking up.

"My dad owns that magazine."

Madison's eyes flick up and shine with the tiniest bit of interest. "I seriously doubt it."

Vivienne shrugs.

"Um, so do you have your math book with you?" I ask. Mr. Jacobi is starting to wander through the library, stopping at each table to see how things are going. The last thing I need is for him to think I'm not doing anything.

"No." Vivienne shrugs again. "I hate math."

"Oh, I'm sure that's not true," I say. "You probably just don't understand it. I used to not like math either, until . . ." I trail off. Because the truth is, I hated math until Brandon and I got together and he started helping me. And it's not as though I really like it all that much now, either, but at least I don't dread it the way I used to. Of course, now that Brandon and I have broken up, there's nothing to look forward to when it comes to math. Just lots of long problems.

"I. HATE. MATH," Vivienne says.

"So I know you don't have your book with you," Brandon says, "but do you at least have your homework?"

Vivienne sighs like it's some kind of big imposition, then reaches into her bag and pulls out her worksheet. I guess you can't judge a book by its cover. This girl is crazy.

"Okay," Brandon says, nodding as he looks it over. "Fractions. This should be pretty easy."

Madison rolls her eyes. "Ew," she says. "Fractions are so useless. It's, like, what are you going to use them for?" She flicks a page in her magazine and tilts her head to the side. "Of course, you can use it to estimate calories when you're only having half a serving of something."

My mouth drops. Is Madison really telling our student that the only thing fractions are good for is making sure you're not eating too many calories? That's ridiculous, not to mention that she really should not be encouraging a nine-year-old to eat less than one serving of anything. That's how little kids end up with eating disorders. It really is a problem facing our country. It's like we're so evolved in some ways, and so not in others, you know?

But if Vivienne is upset by this, she doesn't show it. She

just nods her head. "I never eat a full serving of anything. Unless it's my protein bar after Pilates. Those are good for muscle repair."

Madison nods, agreeing, and then turns another page.

Brandon and I look at each other across the table, and I can tell we're both thinking the same thing. Madison and Micah are going to be no help at all. I mean, Madison's totally tuned out, and Micah has moved on from bouncing his paper ball to playing soccer with it. Seriously, he's trying to kick it in between two stacks of books, like they're goal-posts or something.

"So, why don't we start on the worksheet?" Brandon tries. "Since that's why you're here."

"No, thanks," Vivienne says sweetly, like that's the end of that.

"Come on," he says, giving her a little grin. "Don't you want to get your homework done?"

"Homework is overrated," she says. "My dad owns a huge media empire, and so I'm already going to be rich. I'm, like, an heiress. You know, like Paris Hilton? So I really don't need any skills." She sighs and then reaches up to smooth her hair. And that's when I see she's wearing a Michael Kors watch. A Michael Kors watch! The same one Madison has, in fact. Do you know how much those things cost? Like two or three hundred dollars. And she's *nine*.

I suddenly realize the library has gotten a lot less

loud. Instead of the boisterous sounds of children running around and chattering excitedly, all I hear now is the soft murmur of voices as the kids work on their homework. Even the boy who was pretending the stuffed dog was peeing on everything has settled down and is working happily.

Mr. Jacobi is just a couple of tables away now. He's beaming down at everyone, like he's personally responsible for everything being a success. Which it isn't, really. I mean, he completely overestimated how many tutors he was going to need. But whatever.

"If you work on your worksheet now," I say sweetly, "then tonight, when you get home from school, you won't have to do it."

"I won't have to do it anyway," Vivienne says, her fingers flying over her phone as she texts. I look around wildly for a teacher. Shouldn't someone take her phone away from her? I find it very hard to believe that this is how kids are allowed to act in elementary school.

"Of course you will," Brandon says, still keeping his patience. "It's your homework."

"So what? No one cool does their homework. Like, at all."

Unfortunately, this is kind of true. A lot of the popular kids at my school either don't hand in their homework or just have someone else do it for them. I wonder if I should start lecturing Vivienne about the importance of getting your work done and behaving in a manner that has integrity.

"I'm cool, and I do my homework," I say.

Across the table Madison snorts and then flips a page of her magazine.

"If you do your homework, you'll be able to get good grades," Brandon points out to Vivienne. "And if you get good grades, you'll be able to go to college and be whatever you want. Maybe you'll be a famous mathematician."

Vivienne's eyes are starting to glaze over. She looks away and begins to study her nails. Wow. I can't believe a nine-year-old has a gel manicure. I've always wanted a gel manicure, but they're way more expensive than the regular ones. Plus Micah's mom's salon doesn't offer them. I wonder if I should bring that up to her. I don't think their business is doing too well. And even though Micah is a big pain in the butt, I do like his mom, Sharon. She's always been really nice to me.

I sigh. This day is a huge disaster.

I don't know what to do. Brandon shrugs, like he's out of ideas.

"Or you could become a famous publicist or something," I say. "And you could, like, tour with boy bands. Doing all their publicity. And you'd get super-rich and get to meet them all."

Vivienne perks up for a minute, but then she shakes her head. "I told you, I don't have to go to college," she says. "I have a trust fund. And if I want to meet famous people, all I have to do is ask my dad. He's probably going to get One Direction to play at my thirteenth birthday party."

I want to tell her that by the time she's thirteen, One Direction will be completely over, and *anyone* will be able to get them to play at their party, so she shouldn't feel all special. But then I notice Mr. Jacobi leaving the table next to us and moving toward ours.

Vivienne's paper is completely blank. Great. I rack my brains, trying to come up with something, *anything*, that might get Vivienne to do her work.

"Listen," Madison says, snapping her magazine shut. She leans forward across the table toward Vivienne, so close that their noses are almost touching. Vivienne looks taken aback. I'm taken aback too. I mean, it's pretty aggressive. "I am not going to fail math just because you're too lazy to do some dumb fractions worksheet with"—her eyes flutter down to the paper—"ten stupid problems. Suck it up and do it."

Vivienne narrows her eyes back at Madison. She's obviously not used to being talked to like this. "No," she says. And then, just in case we forgot she's only nine and still a child, she adds, "And you can't make me."

Madison's lips scrunch up into a little smile. It's actually pretty scary. And then I realize there's no way that Vivienne is a match for Madison. I mean, think about it. Madison has had *years* of practicing her brattiness. No way she's going to be taken down by a nine-year-old.

"Do your homework," Madison says, "and I'll let you read my magazine."

Vivienne's eyes widen. That magazine is like some kind of forbidden fruit to her. It's so weird how parents are always telling their kids not to do things, when if they were smart, they'd realize that keeping their kid away from something just makes the kid want it more.

"You'll let me read it?" Vivienne asks, considering.

"No, I'll let you *have* it," Madison says. She leans back and crosses her hands on top of the magazine. "Then you can show all your little friends."

Vivienne thinks about it. Her instinct is to be a brat and tell Madison no way. But she wants that magazine so bad. I can almost see the struggle going on inside her.

"I don't think we should do that," Brandon says. "If her parents don't want her reading the magazine, then we shouldn't give it to her."

He's not trying to use reverse psychology or anything. Brandon's a good person—he really is saying that he doesn't think it's a good idea to bribe Vivienne.

But his remark is enough to push Vivienne over the

edge. The thought of her parents not wanting her to have that magazine is enough to make her want it even more.

"Deal," she says. She picks up her pencil and starts to scribble away at the problems. I glance over her shoulder. Wow. She's actually very good at fractions. She's not even asking for help. I wonder why she's enrolled in tutoring, but then I realize it's probably because she just refuses to do her work, not because she's not capable. She's done with most of the problems in, like, a minute. And from what I can see, they're all correct.

And it's a good thing, too, because Mr. Jacobi is arriving at our table.

"Wonderful," he says, beaming down at us. "Just wonderful." That's the nicest thing Mr. Jacobi's ever said to me. He even pats me on my shoulder as he walks by.

"Done," Vivienne says a few moments later. She sets her pencil down and then holds her hand out. "Give me the magazine."

Madison rolls her eyes, like she can't believe Vivienne is being so demanding. Which is funny, since Madison is the most demanding person I know. "We have to check your homework first," she says. "To make sure it's right."

Micah is back at the table now.

"Micah," Madison commands, "check her work."

"I'll check it," Brandon says quickly, pulling the sheet across the table toward him. Even though Micah is an eighth grader, Brandon obviously doesn't trust him to know what he's doing. And he's probably right not to. Even if Micah is good at math (which I don't know if I believe or not), he definitely wouldn't do a thorough job. The kid spent the last half hour playing soccer with a wadded-up piece of paper.

"Looks good to me," Brandon says after a minute. He passes me the paper. "What do you think, Kendall?"

My face flushes in pleasure, not only that Brandon's actually talking to me but that he has enough faith in my math abilities to ask me for my opinion.

I look the paper over.

"Come on," Vivienne whines. "We don't have all day."

Madison snorts, like this is the funniest joke ever.

"Looks right," I say, giving Vivienne her paper back.

"Gimme," Vivienne says.

Madison takes her time handing Vivienne the magazine. Vivienne runs her fingers over the cover, like she's got some sort of precious jewel or something.

"So, what are we supposed to do now?" Micah asks. He flicks his makeshift ball off the table and onto the ground. "I'm bored of playing ball."

Madison gets a wicked grin on her face. "Let's play truth or dare," she says.

"I don't think that's a good idea," I say, glancing pointedly at Vivienne. Not to mention we're at school. Who plays truth or dare at school? That's ridiculous.

"What's wrong?" Madison asks. "You scared?" And then I realize why she's so enthusiastic about playing. She probably wants to ask me all kinds of embarrassing questions, like if I want to kiss Micah or if Brandon was my first boyfriend. (No and yes.)

"I'm not scared," I say. "I just—"

"Good," she says. "Then truth or dare?"

"Madison," Brandon says, looking uncomfortable. "Come on."

"I'll play," Micah says. "I love dares."

"I'm not asking you," Madison says, all irritated. "I'm asking Kendall."

"When my friends and I play truth or dare, we do ding-dong dash in my neighborhood," Vivienne reports. She sounds proud, like this is some kind of huge accomplishment we should all be impressed with.

Everyone ignores her.

"Kendall," Madison repeats. "Truth or dare."

I swallow, not exactly sure what to do. If I refuse to play, everyone will think it's because I'm afraid of being humiliated. If I pick truth, Madison's going to ask me some totally personal and humiliating question, probably about Brandon. If I pick dare, she's going to dare me to do something equally ridiculous, like kiss Micah in the library in front of everyone.

Micah's drumming his fingers on the table, bored, and Brandon's looking down at his notebook, like he's embarrassed for me. I don't know what to do.

But I'm sick of not doing anything, and I'm sick of being afraid of Madison. So before I even know what's happening, I say, "Dare."

Madison looks surprised, but then her face curls into an evil smile. "I dare you to tell us what really happened between you and Brandon."

"Madison," Brandon says sharply. "Knock it off."

"Why?" Madison opens her eyes all wide and innocent. "What's so bad about it? I mean, she broke up with you, right? Because she likes Micah."

Brandon looks away again, down at the floor.

"Right," Micah says proudly, puffing out his chest.

"You guys used to be boyfriend-girlfriend?" Vivienne asks, looking interested for the first time since she got here.

"So answer it," Madison says.

I swallow hard. Obviously, Brandon isn't going to correct her. He's too nice to tell her what really happened. And if I wanted to, I could call Madison out and say that her dare doesn't count, because really, it's more of a truth. If I wanted to, I could come up with lots of excuses and lies.

But I don't.

Because something happens in that moment. I get sick of lying. I get sick of hiding things. I get sick of pretending to be something that I'm not.

I mean, look where all the lying and pretending has gotten me. Nowhere.

So before I know it, I'm saying, "Brandon and I broke up for a personal reason," I say.

"Duh," Madison says. "That's why it's called a dare. If it's not at least a little personal, then who would care?"

"I'm not going to say what the reason was," I say, "because that's between me and Brandon. But I will say that I never meant for things to end the way they did, and that I still care about him a lot."

My voice catches on that last part, and I'm looking down at my folder, not trusting myself to look up. I don't want to have to see what Brandon's reaction is, and I don't want to have to see Madison's face either.

And then, just when I feel like maybe I can't take it anymore, that I'm going to *have* to look up to see if I can tell what Brandon thinks about what I just said, Mr. Jacobi calls our attention to the front of the library.

I turn around in my chair and look at Mr. Jacobi, and blink back my tears, hoping I'm not going to start crying right here in front of everyone.

"Today was a grand success," Mr. Jacobi says. "Please say good-bye to your students and then follow me outside to begin our walk back to the middle school."

The library explodes into a cacophony of voices and chairs scraping across the floor. But I don't bother to say good-bye to Vivienne, or anyone else. Instead, I just push my chair back and head for the exit.

Chapter 10

I'm the first person on my late bus, and so I choose a seat all the way toward the back. It's starting to get dark, and the light from the streetlights bounces off the dusting of snow that's coating the streets.

I thought maybe Micah would try to sit with me, but he doesn't. Maybe he's mad at me for denying he's the reason I broke up with Brandon. Or he could be sitting up front for some other reason. You never really know with that kid.

As the bus pulls out of the parking lot, Lily appears beside me. She doesn't say anything, maybe because she senses that I need quiet. I find her presence comforting. Even though no one else can see her, it makes me feel like I'm not completely alone.

When I step off the bus at the corner of my street, my boots make footprints in the snow. I breathe the cold air, and my nose tingles. Fall is turning to winter, and in a couple of weeks I probably won't be able to go outside without wearing my hat and gloves.

When I get to my house, my dad's truck is parked on the right side of the driveway, and there's a car I don't recognize sitting next to it. It's not Cindy's old green Camry but a dark gray sedan.

Probably one of my dad's clients, or maybe an architect coming over to go over some plans. Usually my dad meets with clients at job sites, but every so often one of them will come over to meet with him at the house.

I breathe a sigh of relief as I step inside and hang my coat up in the closet. Usually I'd just throw it on the bench in the entranceway, but if my dad has company, I don't want them thinking his daughter is a complete slob. Besides, now that my dad's busy with work, I can sneak upstairs and not have to deal with the fact that he's upset with me.

"That must be Kendall," I hear my dad say from the kitchen. Usually he meets with people in the living room, but whatever.

I move from our entranceway toward the kitchen, figuring I should probably at least say hello to whoever it is who's here.

But when I get to the kitchen, it takes me a second to process what's going on. There are two people sitting at the table, a plate of scones and two mugs sitting in front of them. One of them is my dad, and the other one is a woman with her back to me.

"Hi," I say politely as I move closer. "I'm—"

And then the woman turns around.

And I realize there's no need to introduce myself.

Because the person sitting in the kitchen isn't a client.

It's my mom.

"Oh," I say. "It's you." Which is obviously not my wittiest comment, but I'm so surprised that it's the first thing that comes out.

"Kendall," my dad says. "Do you want to sit down?"

"Not really," I say, finding my voice.

"Are you sure?" he asks. "Because I think there's a lot to talk about."

I don't look at my mom. "What is she doing here?" I ask my dad. First he was talking to her behind my back, and now he has just let her into our house. You'd think he'd have some loyalty. My mom left us. He can't just be letting her into our *home*.

"It's not his fault," my mom says. She wraps her hands around her mug, the same way she did the other day at her house. It must be something she does when she's nervous. It makes me wonder what other things I don't know about her. "I came without telling him."

"So now you can leave without telling him," I say.

"Kendall," my dad says warningly. "Be careful what you—"

"No, it's okay," my mom says. She takes a deep breath. "I understand you're angry at me, Kendall. And I'd like . . . I mean, I'd like a chance to explain."

"I don't want to listen," I say. But even as I'm saying the words, I'm not sure they're true. The thing is, my mom is the only other person, at least that I know of, who can see ghosts. She's the only other person who could possibly understand what it is I'm going through. Maybe she could explain some of it to me, or at the very least give me some insight on how to deal with it.

"Kendall," my dad starts again. "If you don't want to talk to your mother, that's fine. But at least be respectful."

I want to yell that I shouldn't have to be respectful to someone who just abandoned our family, but instead I just sigh. "Fine," I say, crossing my arms over my chest. "I'll give her ten minutes."

"I'll give you two some privacy," my dad says, standing up.

"No, that's okay," my mom says. "We'll go for a walk."

My dad looks at me, asking me silently if that's okay. It makes me happy to know that no matter what has gone on, my dad still has my back. If I don't want to go for a walk with my mom, he'll support me in that decision.

"It's fine," I say. "Let's go for a walk."

I'll take her to the cemetery.

Maybe that will get her in the mood to talk about ghosts.

"It's snowing again," my mom says as we walk across the street.

"Mmm-hmm." I really want to see the flakes falling, but I don't want to give her the satisfaction, so I keep my eyes on the ground. Our steps fall into a rhythm, matching each other's cadence, and I wonder if it's because she's my mom or if it's just one of those random things that would happen with anyone.

When we get to my favorite spot in the cemetery, I stop for a moment, mostly out of habit, but she keeps walking.

She turns around. "You okay?"

I open my mouth to tell her that I usually stop at this bench, that I usually sit here and do my thinking, that this is one of my favorite places to be in the whole world. But something inside me isn't ready for her to be at this place with me. Definitely not now, maybe not ever.

"Yeah, I'm okay," I say. I quicken my step to catch up with her.

"I used to come here all the time before you were born," she says. She pulls the scarf she's wearing a little tighter around her neck. "I used to walk around the paths for hours."

"That's nice," I say, not even trying to keep the edge out of my voice.

She glances over at me. "I know you're angry with me, Kendall."

"Really?" I ask sarcastically. "What would have ever given you that idea?"

She has the sense not to answer. "Your father doesn't know about the ghosts." It's a statement, not a question.

"No."

"You never told him?"

"No."

"So you've been carrying this all by yourself?"

"Yes."

"You never told anyone? Ever?"

"I told . . . I only told Brandon." I move my eyes from the ground to straight ahead, just in case I start crying. If I do, hopefully the snowflakes hitting my face will mask the tears.

My mom's lips settle into a tight line. "Well, I suppose at some point you were going to tell someone." She takes a deep breath." Kendall, I . . . I want you to know that I didn't leave you because I wanted to."

I laugh. "Oh, please," I say. "Save it."

She looks like she's been slapped. "Save it?"

"Yeah. Save it for someone who cares." I can't believe I just said that. I'm not the type of person to say things like that, especially not to my mom.

I expect her to yell at me, or at least tell me not to disrespect her like that, but she doesn't. All she says is, "Well, I guess I deserve that."

"You do," I say, tears filling my eyes. "You left me. You *left* me. I was just a baby, Mom. How could you have done that?"

"You don't understand," she says, stopping and taking a step toward me. I can see the pain etched on her face, and for a second I feel bad for her. But just for a second. "I thought I was going to ruin you. I thought that if I stayed, if I was involved in your life in any way, I'd end up making a mess of things."

"More of a mess than if you left?" I'm almost yelling now. "I needed a mom. I needed someone to explain everything to me, to be there for me! I had no idea where you were, why you left. And now I find out that you were just a couple of hours away, that you've been talking to dad this whole time, that you could have come back anytime you wanted to!"

I don't even know what I'm saying now. All I know is that I'm upset and angry and crying, and it's like every emotion I have about this whole stupid situation with Brandon and Ellie and everything is all coming down on my mom. My life is a mess, and whether it's true or not, I feel like it's all her fault.

"Kendall," she says, stepping toward me again.

"No," I say, stepping back. I stumble a little and almost fall to the ground, but then I catch myself on the edge of a bench. "Don't."

"Kendall, please. You almost fell. Are you—"

"I'm *fine.*" I stand up, still a little unsteady. But I don't care. I don't want to hear about how she's so sorry and how she wants to explain things to me and how she was just trying to protect me and how it hurt her too.

I just want to go home.

So I turn around and run.

I run back through the cemetery, and my boots slip on the soft, wet snow. But I keep going, not caring if I fall.

When I get to my house, I push against the door, stumbling into the hallway.

My dad's there, already waiting. He must have been looking out the window, watching for me.

I collapse against him.

"It's okay, it's okay," he soothes, stroking my hair as I cry.

"Dad," I say, pulling away. "I'm so sorry. For everything."

"It's okay, it's okay," he keeps saying.

Finally, after what feels like forever but is probably only a few minutes, I pull back and wipe my tears from my face. "Can I just go upstairs?" I ask. "Please? I don't know if I can talk about this right now. And I don't . . . I don't want to see her again tonight."

"Of course."

So I go upstairs and wash my face and brush my teeth and then pull my hair back with a headband. When I come out of the bathroom, I peek out the window. My mom's car is gone.

I don't know what my dad said to her before she left, and at this point I really don't care.

My head hurts from crying, and even though I splashed cold water on my skin, my eyes are all puffy.

I curl up in bed, waiting for my dad to come upstairs to talk to me, but a second later I fall asleep.

When I wake up the next morning, there's a fresh blanket over me. My dad must have tucked me in.

Chapter 11

We don't talk about it.

Any of it—not about what happened with my mom, not about me getting in trouble at school, nothing.

At least not at first.

My dad tries. But I'm just not ready.

So he tells me he'll be there to talk when I want to, and until then he'll give me space so I can process what's been going on. Not that I really know how to process anything. I mean, I'm only twelve. Processing sounds like something that takes a long time and involves lot of emotional unrest.

And I'm more of a live-in-the-moment kind of girl. At least I have been until now. Maybe processing things is what you have to do when you start to grow up. Either way, I'm going to have to figure it out soon, because at some point I'm sure my dad's going to get over the whole being-patient-with-me thing.

The next few days pass in a blur. We're tackling a new unit in math, and so I have my hands full trying to keep up. Ellie and I are talking more, but it's weird because she's spending a lot of time with Kyle and Brandon, and obviously I can't hang out with her when they're around.

So I spend my lunch periods in the library, working on my math.

After school I watch movies in my room. (My dad surprised me by getting a new TV delivered. I know it's kind of a pity gift, but I don't care. I'm not sure if watching a lot of reruns of ABC Family in high-def luxuriousness really counts as processing, but I decide to pretend that it does.)

Of course, I still have Lily to deal with. She's been very patient with me the past couple of days, not even getting upset when I spend more time processing than I do helping her move on. Most ghosts definitely wouldn't have been so understanding.

So by the time Saturday morning rolls around, I figure I owe it to her to take the next step.

The next step means I'm going to have to find a way to get to Sadler State. I MapQuest it, and it turns out the college is only about fifteen miles away. Yes, it's a long way, but I'm pretty sure I can bike there.

One time me and Ellie biked twenty miles to this karate competition she wanted to go to. (She said it was because she was thinking about getting into martial arts, but I'm pretty sure it was because she had a crush on this kid who was going to be competing. She didn't want to admit it to me, because he was kind of a jerk. He wasn't even that cute, either, but he had red hair, and Ellie's a sucker for redheads.)

"So do you remember what dorm you were in?" I ask Lily on Saturday morning.

My dad is working today, finishing up a job that's way behind schedule, so I don't have to worry about him asking me where I'm going.

Lily closes her eyes and scrunches up her adorable little nose. "Yes," she says. "Millbank Hall."

"Okay." I try to keep the skepticism out of my voice. Apparently Lily suddenly remembers her dorm, which I'm happy about, but I'm also trying not to get too excited. I mean, until recently she didn't even know she was in college. So obviously her memories are a little faulty.

"Do I look like a college student?" I ask her now, twirling around in front of the mirror. I'm wearing my best dark-washed jeans and a crisp white button-down with a gray wool sweater over it. My hair is pulled back in a messy bun. I was going to add a pencil, but I thought maybe that was going too far. Same with the pair of fake glasses I was going to buy.

"Umm . . . you look really nice," Lily says.

"You don't think I could pass for a college student?" I turn this way and that, admiring my look. This outfit definitely makes me look way older than I am. I even put on a smoky eye shadow that my dad never lets me wear to school because he says I'm too young for it. But I'll bet all the girls at college wear makeup like this. I look like I'm at least fifteen. For sure.

"Oh, you definitely could," Lily says, then quickly looks away.

Hmmph. Well, it doesn't matter what she thinks anyway. All that matters is what the people at her school think. Not that I know I'm definitely going to have to pass for a college student. In fact, I'm not sure exactly what I'm going to have to pass for. Maybe I can pretend to be Madison! Probably not, if what Madison says is true and she went to visit Lily at college before. Probably everyone there knows her already. But maybe I can pretend to be Lily's cousin or something.

Anyway, I definitely don't want to plan things out too much. I mean, sometimes if you go into a situation with a preconceived notion, it doesn't work out the way you thought it would.

When I get outside and pull my bike out of the garage, I say a silent whisper of thanks that the weather's nice. It's almost sixty degrees today, even though it was snowing just a few days ago. Welcome to fall in Connecticut.

I hop on my bike and start pedaling.

This won't be that bad, I tell myself. The weather is warm, and how hard can fifteen miles really be? Those riders who do the Tour de France ride something like two hundred miles a day. And yeah, they're professional athletes who are in ridiculously good shape. But if humans can ride two hundred miles a day at top speed, then I should definitely be able to ride fifteen miles at a moderate pace.

Miles one and two are nice.

Miles three and four are on a bit of an incline, but I shift gears and enjoy coasting down the other side.

Miles five through ten definitely seem like they're taking a little longer to get through, but when I check my watch, I see that I'm keeping a steady pace.

By mile ten I think I'm going to die. What I thought was nice bike-riding weather turns out to be way too hot. I'm starting to sweat, and I have to take my sweater off and tie it around my waist. Which is actually good, because my butt is starting to hurt from sitting on my seat, and the sweater provides a nice cushion.

"Isn't this so fun?" Lily asks from the handlebars. "It's such a gorgeous day."

"Yes. So. Fun." I grunt as I push down on the pedals. I'm glad at least one of us is having an easy time of it. Well, as easy as you can have when you're a dead ghost who's trying to take care of some unfinished business and move on to the other side.

When the huge stone sign that says STATE UNIVERSITY OF CONNECTICUT AT SADLER comes into view, I breathe a sigh of relief. I have no idea how I'm going to be able to bike all the way home. I might have to hang out here for a while and wait until the air gets a little cooler.

We bike through the main campus to the admissions building, and then I put the brakes on.

"Where to?" I ask, straddling my bike.

"What do you mean?" Lily asks. She's looking around campus with a smile on her face. "Wow, this place brings back so many memories."

I know I should probably ask her what kind of memories, but I'm not really on the kind of schedule that allows for reminiscing.

So instead I just say, "Where's your dorm?" Hopefully it's not too far. I don't know if my legs can take it.

"My dorm?" She looks around. "Um, I'm not sure."

Great. I guess her newfound college memories don't include directions.

Whatever. It can't be too far. And there's a big stone map of the campus in front of the admissions building.

I walk my bike over there, and Lily and I study it.

Luckily, Millbank Hall is only three buildings over.

"We should probably walk," Lily says. "No one here rides bikes."

I look around. She's right. There are tons of kids milling around, and not one of them is riding a bike. Hmm. And none of them is wearing clothes, either. I mean, they're not *naked* or anything. They're just all in their pajamas.

No wonder Lily didn't think I looked like a college student. I'm way too dressed up to be a college student. And this smoky eye shadow is definitely not appropriate. I guess Saturday mornings are a little more, ah, chill around here.

I decide to leave my bike at the bike rack near the main buildings. Of course, I've forgotten to bring my bike lock, so I'm just going to have to take the chance that no one steals it. I really doubt anyone is going to take my hot-pink ten-speed with sparkly tinsel hanging from the handlebars. (What? Me and Ellie did this to our bikes when we were eleven. It was cool at the time, and if you want to know the truth, I kind of still like it.)

"I hope no one steals your bike," Lily says helpfully.

"Yeah," I say. "Me too."

We follow the winding sidewalk through some trees and over a cute little bridge that leads to the quad. Beyond that I can see the dorms looming in the distance.

"This is a nice walk," Lily says.

"Would have been nicer if I hadn't just biked fifteen miles," I mutter under my breath.

"What?" she asks.

"Nothing," I say cheerfully. A big brick building with MILLBANK HALL on the side has come into view.

Now, how do I get in? The building has big double doors and what looks like a keypad on the outside of it. It definitely looks very secure.

"How do we get in?" I ask Lily.

"I don't know." She looks at me. "Break in through a window?"

"Um, no," I say. "I mean, how did you get in? Is there a key, or a code, or what?"

"I'm not sure," she says. "I don't remember."

I stand and look at the building, hoping someone is going to go in or come out. But although the main campus had some students wandering around, down here by the dorms things are decidedly more quiet.

We sit down on a bench near the side of the building and wait. My legs could use the rest. After about fifteen minutes or so, two boys wearing puffy navy-blue vests and carrying cups of hot coffee come wandering down the path.

"It was so sick," one of them is saying. "The dude, like, broke his arm. And the bone was sticking out."

"That's awesome," the other kid says.

I really have no idea what's so awesome about someone breaking their arm and bones sticking out, but whatev. (Actually, now that I think about it, that sounds exactly like something boys would think is cool. Which is very upsetting, since I was hoping that by the time I got to college, boys would be more mature than they are in seventh grade. But I guess not.)

"There was blood spurting all over the place," the first boy continues. They're walking up the steps to the dorm now, and I sort of meander over there, just in case there's an opportunity for me to slip in the door. "And pus was coming out."

Lily looks at me and raises her eyebrows, and now I know this guy is definitely not telling the truth. Pus was coming out of a broken bone? No way. We learned in science class that pus is caused by a buildup of white blood cells from an infection. And I highly doubt that whoever they're talking about had an infection before they broke their arm. It doesn't make sense. Now, if they said the infection came *after*, then—

Oh! They're opening the door. The lying kid is balancing his coffee in the crook of his arm and has taken out some kind of key card. There's a beep and a whoosh as the door opens and the two of them disappear inside.

I sprint up the stairs and grab the door right before it's about to shut. I slip inside, then glance around furtively, halfway expecting there to be some kind of guard or at least a check-in desk or something. But there's no one.

"Jeez," I say. "This place isn't very secure, is it?"

"That's why we had a lot of break-ins here," Lily says wisely. "They were talking about revamping the security system, but I guess they haven't gotten around to it yet."

Great. Apparently Lily can remember the agenda of the school administration in regard to their security policies, but she can't remember how to get in the building.

I smooth my shirt down and try to look like I belong. Although now that I'm here, I'm nervous. I thought dressing more grown-up would make me not stick out, but I got it all wrong.

I take a deep breath and then head down the hallway. I don't really know where I'm going, but I can't just stand here. Eventually someone's going to walk in, and when they do, they're probably going to ask me what I'm doing. Or even worse, they might demand to know who I am.

I walk around the corner. La, la, la, nothing to see here, just hanging out.

And then I spot the student mailboxes against one wall.

Score! I can look for Lily's name on the mailboxes, and hopefully it will have her room number there as well.

I sidle over and start running my finger over the names. Wow. This is going to take forever. There's probably, like, six hundred mailboxes here, and each one has two names. Each student must share their mailbox with their roommate.

Twenty minutes later I've looked through every name and haven't found Lily's.

They must have removed her name after she died.

"Can you remember your roommate's name?" I ask her hopefully. "Even just, like, an initial or something?"

She shakes her head sadly. "No, I'm sorry."

I take a deep breath and think. How can I find out Lily's roommate's name? There are a few mailboxes that only have one name on them. I assumed they were for the RAs, or the kids who have singles. Maybe Lily's room is one of those. It would make sense—after she died, her roommate probably got to have the room to herself. There's no way the college would move in some new roommate after such a tragedy. That would be, like, totally traumatic.

I guess I could write down all the room numbers that just have single names on their mailboxes, but then what would I do? Go to every single room and knock on the door, asking the person if their roommate died? That would take forever. And I'm kind of pressed for time, now that I realize how long it takes to bike over here.

"Maybe we should check the mailboxes again," Lily's grumbling. She starts pacing the hallway. "Why would they take my name off? That's so messed up. Just because I died doesn't mean that they have to completely forget about me, does it?"

"No." She kind of has a point. Just because she died doesn't mean they have to remove her name from their mailboxes. It's, like, erasing her memory or something. How callous.

The sound of the building door opening echoes through the lobby, and Lily looks at me with alarm. "Quick!" she says. "Look casual!"

I'm not sure how I'm supposed to do that, so I just put my head down and pretend to be looking for something in my bag. I might look nothing like a college student, but hopefully no one will be able to tell this just by looking at the back of my head.

Two girls' voices move down the hallway. I wish it were boys who were coming in. Boys don't care about anything. They're not curious at all. It comes in handy when you have to ask them things and pry around for information.

La, la, la. Oh, nothing, just pretending to look for my keys.

The voices get closer, bringing with them a rush of cool outside air.

I keep rummaging through my bag. Lily, obviously, doesn't have to worry about anything, because she's a ghost. No one can see her, thank God.

The girls are getting closer, and now I can hear their conversation. They're talking about lip gloss or something ridiculous like that. One of the voices actually sounds very familiar. Like, *very* familiar.

In fact, it almost sounds like Madison.

As they pass, I shift my eyes from my bag to the floor.

Wow. The person with the same voice as Madison also

has the same UGG boots as Madison. I know because Madison loves to brag about her dumb sparkly UGG boots and how she got them the day they came out because she knew they were going to be sold out everywhere. Which they are, which kind of makes no sense, because they're not even that great. Well, they *weren't* that great. Now that they're sold out, they're infinitely greater just because they're hard to get.

"I can't believe how fab your hair looks, Madison," the other girl says.

I almost gasp out loud. What are the chances that some girl has the same voice as Madison and the same hard-to-find boots as Madison and the same name as Madison and yet isn't Madison? And that settles it. I can't help it. I look up.

It's Madison.

She's got a scarf around her neck and she's wearing a long, slouchy sweater and skinny jeans, and she looks like a college student. Like what a college student would look like if they got dressed all collegiate and casual. She has a lot less makeup on than she usually does too. Just a swipe of mascara and a little blush.

She looks effortlessly put together. How annoying.

"Your sister would be really proud of you," the girl with Madison is saying. She's wearing jeans too, and a red sweater. She has stick-straight dirty-blond hair, and a soft-looking brown leather messenger bag is slung over her shoulder.

The two of them disappear around the corner, and I breathe a sigh of relief. That could have been a disaster. Could you imagine if Madison had caught me in her sister's dorm? Oh my God, she probably would have called the police or something. Not that I'm doing anything illegal. Although sneaking into a college dorm when you don't live there definitely could be illegal. I'm not really sure, but it could be, like, breaking and entering or something.

"That was Stella," Lily whispers. "That was my roommate. It's so weird. . . . I . . . I recognized her." She looks at me, her eyes wide, and then she rubs her temples, like she's getting a headache from the remembering.

"Come on," I say. "If we hurry, we can catch up to them."

"Why would we want to catch up to them?" Lily asks.

"Because," I say, "they're going to your room. We have to follow them."

Following Madison and Stella turns out to be surprisingly easy, considering they end up in an elevator and me and Lily have to take the stairs in order to catch up with them. (Of course, this is considerably easier for Lily, since she's a ghost and doesn't have to worry about things like bad cardio. Not to mention I'm the one who just biked fifteen miles.)

We don't know what floor the elevator is going to stop

on, but luckily it's super-loud and squeaky. Apparently, most people in this dorm are either at breakfast or still sleeping, because the stairwell and the whole building are very quiet. At the top of each flight, I stop for a second to see if I can still hear the elevator.

By the time we get to the fourth floor, I feel like I might die.

I bend over, trying to catch my breath, and listen for the elevator to stop.

DING!

The sound of the elevator doors opening drifts out to the stairwell, and Lily claps her hands.

"Yes!"

I peer through the pane of glass in the door of the stairwell. On the other side of the door is what looks like a lounge area. There's a bunch of navy-blue upholstered chairs and an oak coffee table and a big flat screen TV. The room is a square, and there's a door in each corner.

Hmmm. If those doors lead to the rooms, I have no idea how I'm going to get inside. Each doorknob has a keypad where you enter a code. How am I supposed to know the code? And besides, it's one thing to sneak into a building. It's another thing altogether to sneak into someone's actual dorm room. Not to mention that if I get caught, it's definitely going to be breaking and entering. You can't just go into someone's—

"I'm so glad you came!" Stella's voice comes trilling through the lounge, followed by Stella herself.

I gasp, and then duck down behind the door.

"Shh!" Lily instructs. "You are a really loud gasper."

I give her an I'm-sorry look.

"It's okay," Lily says. She's still standing and looking through the glass. "Okay. They're walking toward the door that's right across from us."

"Can you see what the code is?" I whisper.

"What code?"

"You need a code to get into the room or the suite or whatever it is," I say. "Can you see what numbers Stella's punching in?"

"I'm not sure," Lily says, sounding doubtful. She pushes her nose right up against the glass. "Hold on." She floats through the door.

Her being invisible and able to move through solid objects is really coming in handy right now. I stay pushed up against the wall, my fingers crossed behind my back, hoping Lily can find the code before someone comes out here and finds me. I try to come up with a story about what I'm doing here, but I can't really think of anything good. There's really no good reason to be hiding in a hallway at a college where I know no one.

Lily comes back a few seconds later, a huge smile on her face. "One, three, two, four," she says. "I got the code."

"Good job!" I jump up and hold my hand out for a high five, but her hand just goes right through mine. We both giggle.

"So now what?" Lily asks.

"Now," I say, sighing, "we have to wait until they leave."

"And then what?"

"Then," I say, "we break in."

Chapter 12

You'd think that Stella and Madison wouldn't be in that room for long, wouldn't you? You'd think that they'd want to get out and do *something*. I mean, what can possibly be so fun about sitting in a dorm room?

Half an hour later my butt is falling asleep and my calves are starting to cramp from sitting.

I stand up and jog in place.

"What are they doing in there?" I grumble.

"Maybe they're telling nice stories about me," Lily says. "You know, like reminiscing."

"Maybe."

I hop from one foot to the other, trying not to let myself get mad at Lily. It's not her fault that I'm stuck out here. It's not really anyone's fault except for Madison's. Why does she have to be in there, talking away, blabbing and blabbing? She's probably not even telling stories about her sister. She's probably telling stories about herself.

My phone vibrates with a text.

Ellie!

Ellie is texting me!

Even though we technically made up, Ellie and I haven't moved on to texting or talking on the phone again. It's nice that she's sending me a text right now.

Want to go to the mall?

And she wants to hang out!

Crap.

We really need to get this show on the road.

I peer through the glass, wondering if maybe I should go and throw something at the door to get their attention.

Or maybe I should send Lily in there to see what they're doing. If they're settling in for a long time, I might have to just come back another day. I know I'm already here and everything, but there's no use wasting my time if—

Just then the door to the suite comes flying open.

I hit the deck. Ew. This floor is incredibly dirty. Someone really should clean it. Don't they have, like, cleaning people to do that kind of thing? Or are the students in charge of doing it themselves? They really should have cleaning people, especially with all the tuition hikes that have been going on at state schools. My dad's always complaining about them.

"Thanks for letting me get the rest of Lily's stuff," I can hear Madison saying.

"No problem," Stella says. "Are you sure you have time to eat before your parents pick you up?"

"Totally. I'm starving," Madison says. "All I had to eat today was, like, three fat-free Swedish Fish."

I resist the urge to roll my eyes.

"Well, the dining hall has the best pancakes," Stella says. "It's one of the only things they don't ruin."

"Ew," Madison says. "Pancakes are so fattening."

"Calories on Saturday mornings don't count," Stella says, and the two of them giggle before the sound of their voices disappears down the hall.

"Good," I say, breathing a sigh of relief. "They should be gone for a little while." Now I just have to make sure I don't get caught breaking and entering. "Come on," I tell Lily. "We're going in."

Sure enough, Lily had the code right. Once I punch the code into the keypad, the door of the suite swings right open. We walk into a main sitting area that has three more doors off it. Which means the suite has three rooms—one for Stella and Lily, and two for whoever else lives in it.

The suite is completely quiet. So either the roommates in the other two rooms are out or, more likely, they're sleeping. And I'd really like to keep it that way. Hopefully, we can get in and out before anyone sees us.

I'm about to ask Lily if she remembers which room is hers when I notice there are construction paper cutouts on each door in the shape of stars. Each one has a name written on it.

The door to my left says "Stella" on one and "Lily" on the other. It's one of those things they probably do before everyone gets to school to make it seem welcoming. Normally I would think that kind of thing is super-cheesy, but now I'm thankful.

I tiptoe over to the door and put my hand on the doorknob.

"It'll be unlocked," Lily says. "Stella never locks her door."

I hold my breath and hope she's right. I turn the knob. It opens.

"Oh my God," I breathe. "We're in."

I push the door open.

The room is neat and tidy, with two single beds, two desks, and two closets in the far wall. A purple shag rug sits on the floor, and the walls are filled with posters, mostly of Nicholas Sparks movies.

"Oh, God," Lily says. "I totally forgot about Stella's

obsession with Nicholas Sparks." She stops in front of the poster for *The Lucky One*. "Although I don't mind the one with Zac Efron so much."

"Okay," I say, anxious to get going. "So what are we looking for?"

"The balcony?" she suggests.

Against one wall there's a pair of light purple billowy curtains in front of a sliding glass door.

"Wow," I say as I move closer. "Whoever designed these dorm rooms really wasn't that smart. Why would they give college students balconies when everyone knows there's a chance the students are going to fall off them?"

But Lily doesn't answer me. She's just looking out onto the balcony with a stricken expression on her face.

"We don't have to do this, you know," I say, even though it's a lie. We kind of do have to do this. If she backs out now, I'm not sure when we're going to get the chance to come back. But if she feels pressure, she might freak out, so I'm going to pretend like this isn't a big deal.

"No, I'm okay," she says.

Thank God.

I push the sliding glass door open and step out onto the balcony. I hope this thing isn't, like, compromised or anything. It feels sturdy, but you never know—I mean, Lily did fall off it.

Hmm. There's definitely not much of a view from here. All you can see is the other building across the path. Another dorm. And the balcony is pretty small. There's a very tiny table and chairs out here, but there's not any room for anything else. I can hardly move. No wonder Lily fell.

I hope someone started a petition or something to remove these balconies. Although I'm not sure how you would remove them. I mean, they're stuck on. But still. There has to be a way. Maybe I should mention it to my dad. I bet it would be a huge project for his construction company, and I'll bet he would get—

"There's nothing out here!" Lily says, looking around. "There's nothing. . . . I mean, I thought there would be something important or that I would at least *remember* something. But I don't. I don't even remember falling."

"Well, give it a second," I say. "Maybe you just need to relax and let it come to you."

"Okay." But she doesn't seem convinced. We stand there for a few moments, waiting to see if she remembers anything.

I pull my phone out and text Ellie back.

What time are you going to the mall?

If I can get this over with quickly, maybe I can meet up with her.

"Maybe there's something else in the room," Lily says

finally. "I just . . . I don't know. I'm not really feeling it out here."

I resist the urge to point out that she hasn't really been feeling things anywhere lately, but I don't. There's no need to be mean about it.

"Okay," I say. "Um, maybe we should go back inside?"

She nods. We walk back into the room, and she looks around.

"Anything?" I ask.

"Sort of." She shrugs. "I don't know. This place seems familiar, but it feels more like . . . I don't know, like it's some kind of dream or something. Like a place I used to know but don't anymore, if that makes sense."

"That makes total sense," I say.

Lily walks over to one of the twin beds, the one that's against the far wall. It's made up in a Creamsicle-colored bedspread. While the other bed is disheveled, like whoever slept in it didn't make it, this one is made so perfectly, it looks like it should be in a hotel room. It even has these super-cute orange-and-white-striped throw pillows.

"This was my bed," she says. "I used to sleep here."

She sits down and slides all the way across until her back is against the wall. "I remember!" She's grinning happily. "Maybe if I stay here longer, I'll remember something else!"

"That's great," I say, not wanting to discourage her. I hope whatever it is she's planning on remembering she does in, oh, about twenty minutes or so. I'm assuming that's about how long it will take Madison and Stella to finish their pancakes. Of course, it could take them a lot longer, but who wants to take chances?

"Yup," Lily says. Her eyes have a faraway look in them.

I make my way over to one of the desks in the corner and sit down. If this is going to take a while, I might as well be comfy. There are pages and books spread out all over the place. College work looks hard. I'll bet my seventh-grade math is nothing compared to this stuff.

"God, this is so weird," Lily's saying. "I can remember sitting here. I can remember working on my homework in this bed. I can remember writing here." She takes a deep breath and closes her eyes. "And I think . . . I think I can remember falling. I was leaning over, trying to look at a flower or something, and I leaned too far and just . . . lost my balance." Her eyes fly open. "I remember something else, too." She gets a weird look on her face, the kind of look you get when you've remembered something you don't want to remember.

She slides her hand down between the bed and the wall and pulls out a spiral notebook. The fact that she can do this is crazy—ghosts are usually not that powerful. She must have gotten a surge of energy, which means that whatever she found is probably very, very important.

The front of the notebook is covered with printed-out pictures. Flowers, cartoon hearts, pictures of Lily and Stella, a picture of a mountain.

"What's that?" I ask.

"This is my journal," she breathes. "This is . . ." She trails off and starts flipping through the pages. "Oh my God," she says. "This is the reason I needed to come back."

"To get your journal?"

She nods. "My mom and I . . . we had a fight right before I died. We made up, but I wrote all this horrible stuff about her in here. If she ever found it, if she ever read it, it would kill her."

Lily's crying now, the tears sliding down her cheeks slowly as she reads through her journal. "We need to destroy this," she says. "Or at least take it somewhere that my mom will never find it."

"Good idea," I say. I gesture to the side of the room, where there's an incense stick and a book of matches sitting on a nightstand. "Should we burn it?"

Lily wrinkles her nose. "Isn't that kind of dangerous? We're not even supposed to have incense in the dorms. In fact, the only reason that's even there is because Stella insists on having it. It's ridiculous." She stops and looks at me, a huge smile on her face. "Wow," she says. "I'm remembering things left and right."

"Yeah, you're right," I say. "Maybe we should bury it or something."

"No!" She shakes her head. "I want it gone. And I want it gone now. We have to burn it."

But now that she's suddenly on board, I'm rethinking this plan. "What if we set off the fire alarm? Or what if someone smells the burning?"

"We're not going to set off the fire alarm," she says. "And we'll be gone before anyone smells anything. Come on. It won't even take that long. We'll do it in the trash can. There are bottles of water in the fridge so we can douse it after."

I sigh. "Fine," I say. "But if I get arrested for arson . . ." I trail off, because honestly, there's not much I can threaten her with. She's already dead. And besides, if this works, she'll be gone.

She grins and watches as I take the journal and rip out each page, tossing them one by one into the metal garbage can. Then I take the empty covers and light the corner of one with a match and drop it on top of the pages. This is actually kind of disappointing.

"Wow," I say. "I thought there was going to be some kind of big inferno."

We both stand there watching the pages burn and the flames die out until there's nothing left but a few ashes. Then I grab the bottle of water and pour a little on the embers, just to make sure it's safe.

"Phew," I say, standing up. "Now let's get the heck out of here."

But when I look up, Lily is gone.

Well. That settles that. Another ghost gone to the other side. I can't help but feel a little happy with myself. I mean, even though I had tons of personal problems going on, and even though Lily was the sister of my archenemy, I was able to put everything aside and help her.

Of course, now I just have to get out of here.

I'm on my way back down the stairs when I hear the *ding* of the elevator. And then I hear Madison's voice going, "Ew, it smells like burnt popcorn in here."

I'm still trying to keep from laughing when I get back to my bike.

I'm in such a good mood that I don't even mind the bike ride home. It's actually kind of nice.

Ellie texts me back, and we make plans to meet at the mall later.

So when I get inside and see my dad sitting at the table, eating a grilled cheese sandwich, I don't feel like I should avoid him. In fact, I feel like I want to sit down and talk to him.

"Hey," I say.

"Hi."

"How was work?" I ask.

"It was good." He doesn't ask me where I was, which I'm thankful for. I'm not sure what I would say to him at this point.

"So," he says, clearing his throat. "Uh, would you like a grilled cheese?"

My dad is a pretty good cook, and one of his specialties is grilled cheese sandwiches. "Can I have bacon on it?" I ask, grinning.

"Of course."

I sit down at the kitchen table and pull the sleeves of my sweater down over my hands as my dad starts assembling the ingredients for the sandwich. It's a bit awkward, just sitting here with nothing to do, so I decide to make myself a hot chocolate.

I get up and grab a mug and fill it with water, then pop it into the microwave.

"So should we talk about what's been going on?" my dad asks as he butters two pieces of bread for my sandwich.

"I'd like to," I say, taking a deep breath. "But first I want to say that I'm really sorry for skipping class. That was not cool of me. I was . . . Me and Ellie were in a fight, and I know that's not an excuse, but I wanted to talk to her. It felt more important than class at the time."

"And I owe you an apology," he says. "I shouldn't have let your mother into the house like that the other day. But she showed up here wanting to talk, and I felt like I owed it to her to listen to what she had to say."

There's a sizzle as he places three pieces of bacon into the frying pan.

"Why?" I ask. "Because she's my mom?"

He nods. "Yes. And because you'd gone to see her, and so I thought . . . I don't know what I was thinking. I should have asked you if it was okay."

"Yes," I agree. "You should have."

"Call it a draw?" he offers. "You forgive me for that, and I'll forgive you for skipping class?"

I pull my mug out of the microwave and mix a hot chocolate packet into the hot liquid. "Really?"

"Well, provided you don't do it again."

"I won't," I promise. "Getting detention is enough of a punishment, trust me."

He nods.

I sit back down at the kitchen table and wait until he sets the sandwich down in front of me. I take a moment to inhale the delicious scent. After my huge bike ride, I'm totally ravenous.

"Listen," my dad says. "I want you to know that I'm going to support you always, no matter what. I want you to know that just because your mother was here the other day doesn't mean you have to let her into your life. That's your decision, and no one else's. If you don't want to see her, that's your prerogative."

"Thanks, Dad," I say. "I really appreciate that." I take a bite of my sandwich, letting the warm cheese and buttered bread warm my soul. Paired with the creamy hot chocolate, it's the perfect meal to have while making up with your dad.

"And I also want you to know that I know I'm not the best with feelings and emotions, but if there are things you want to talk to me about, I'm always here. No matter what."

This last part makes me tear up a bit. I know it couldn't have been easy on my dad, being a single parent. And now that I'm a teenager, I'm sure it's even harder.

"Thank you, Dad," I say again. "That really means a lot to me."

He reaches over and squeezes my hand, and I squeeze back.

"So," he says, taking a bite of his own sandwich and washing it down with a sip of water, "did you and Ellie make up?"

"I think so," I say. "I mean, I'm not exactly sure, but she did just text me and invite me to go to the mall with her later." I fiddle with the hair tie that's around my wrist. I know my dad said we could call it a draw, but I'm not sure if he meant it would be completely forgiven and that I'm not grounded or something. "So can I go?"

He glances at the clock on the microwave. "I can drop

you off at five," he says. "If Ellie's mom can have you home by nine, I think that would be fine."

I text Ellie the latest, and she texts me back a few seconds later, agreeing.

Things are looking up!

Chapter 13

The mall is ridiculously crowded because it's Saturday night, and it turns out there's some kind of dance going on at the high school next week, so all the clothes stores are filled with girls looking for dresses and freaking out.

Ellie and I spend some time in Justice, browsing and trying on clothes. She buys a really cute lacy black shirt, and I buy some bangle bracelets and a sparkly red headband.

Then we head over to the food court, where we plan on getting some Japanese food from the make-your-own stir-fry place. Seriously, it's sooo good. As long as you don't think about what really goes into it. I mean, it definitely can't be good for you. You can practically see the grease pooling at the bottom of the Styrofoam containers they give you.

Next to the Japanese place is one of those toy stores that have all kinds of crazy toys—like remote control planes and stuff.

We're standing in line to get our food when all of a sudden one of the helicopters lands right in front of us.

"What the . . . ," Ellie says. "Oh!" she says, brightening. "It's Kyle!"

I turn around, and sure enough, there's Kyle. He's standing there, holding the remote for the helicopter and looking mischievous.

"Hey," he says, giving Ellie a quick kiss on the cheek.

"Hey," she says. "I thought you were at your cousin's birthday party."

"I was," he says. "But then it ended early, and so I decided to come to the mall for a little while."

"Cool," Ellie says.

Great. Just great. Now that Kyle is here, I'm going to be the third wheel. Which, let's face it, isn't really that fun. Me and Ellie were having such a good time, too. It was just like old times. I wonder if this is how it's going to be from now on—me hanging with Ellie and Kyle, always the odd man out.

Or what if Ellie and Kyle start hanging out with Madison

and Brandon? Oh my God! That would be the worst thing ever. Sure, Ellie says she doesn't like Madison, but Madison can be very manipulative and persuasive. Not that I think Ellie is easily manipulated, but—

"Hey," a voice says next to me. "Um, I think it's your turn to order."

I turn around. Ohmigod. It's Brandon. Brandon is here at the mall! Brandon is here at the mall with Kyle, not out with Madison!

"Uh," I say brilliantly. "What?"

"It's your turn," he says, then points to where the guy behind the counter is staring at me impatiently.

"Oh." I turn around to give my order. "Um, I'll have chicken teriyaki."

"Make it two," Brandon says.

Ellie is standing in line behind us, with Kyle. The two of them are talking about the birthday party Kyle went to, but every so often Ellie gives me a furtive glance. I can tell she's wondering whether or not I'm okay with Brandon being here.

Am I okay? I don't know. I mean, I *like* him being here, but are we going to talk? So far we're not talking. So far we're just standing here, waiting for our food.

The man puts two Styrofoam containers filled with chicken, rice, and veggies up on the counter.

"Can we have extra sauce?" Brandon asks.

I flush with pleasure. He remembered I like extra sauce! He wouldn't have remembered that if he didn't care about me, would he? Although, Brandon is a very nice person. He definitely could just be being polite.

"You know what?" I hear Ellie announce loudly. "I don't think I want Japanese food after all."

"What?" I ask, surprised. "You kept talking about how bad you were dying for it." Ellie's a vegetarian, and so that veggie bowl with rice is one of the only things she can eat in the mall food court.

"Yeah, I know," she says, "but now I think I'm more in the mood for pizza." She turns to Kyle. "You wanna go get pizza?"

"Sure," Kyle says. He's always up for pizza.

"We'll be right back," Ellie says. And then I get it. She wants to give me and Brandon some time alone, so she's leaving, and she's taking Kyle with her!

But I don't want to be alone with Brandon. I mean, that's so awkward. What are we going to talk about? Besides, the last thing I want to seem is desperate. He broke up with me.

"Are you sure?" I ask desperately. "Because the food here is really good."

But Ellie just waves and then takes Kyle's hand and pulls him down toward the pizza place.

Brandon and I lapse into an awkward silence.

I should say something. But what? I've never been good

at small talk. That's why even though Brandon sat ahead of me in math class, it took me forever to have a conversation with him.

Luckily, we're at the cash register now, paying for our food, so we're spared from having to talk about anything.

But only for a few minutes.

"So," Brandon says as we look around the food court for open seats. "You want to sit over there?"

"Sure." I follow him to the empty table, weaving in and out of the moms with strollers, squealing high school kids, and families out for some shopping.

"So how's your weekend?" I ask Brandon once we're sitting down.

"Fine," he says, and shrugs. "Kind of boring."

I want to ask him if "kind of boring" involved hanging out with Madison, but I don't.

"That's good," I say. Which makes no sense. Why would it be good that he's having a boring weekend? I quickly take a bite of my food. But I can't even enjoy it. That's how nervous he's making me.

"Are you excited for our next tutoring session?" he asks sarcastically.

"Oh, yeah," I say, just as sarcastically. "I can't wait to bribe children to do their homework."

He laughs. "Did you see the look on Mr. Jacobi's face when he realized that each of the kids had four tutors?"

"Oh my God," I say, laughing. "He was about to lose it."

"I've seen him once like that before," Brandon says. "When he was trying to photocopy our math tests in the office and the copier wouldn't work. He said a swear word and everything."

"No way!"

"Yup."

Brandon and I laugh, and it's like bonding over Mr. Jacobi totally breaks the ice. A few minutes later Ellie and Kyle join us with their pizza, and we all eat together, then spend the rest of the evening wandering around the mall, trying on sunglasses, taking funny pictures of each other on our cell phones, and annoying innocent shop assistants.

It's almost like nothing has changed.

Almost.

Because at the end of the night Brandon doesn't kiss me.

And when I fall asleep that night, all I'm thinking about is how much I wish he had.

On Monday morning I'm in such a good mood that I take extra time to do my hair. I leave most of it loose and flowing around my shoulders but pull one side back into three tiny braids. It's one of my favorite looks, but it takes a long time, so I usually only do it when I'm super-happy.

And honestly, what's to be upset about? Me and my dad

are talking again, Ellie and I are friends, Brandon doesn't seem to hate me, and I helped Lily move on. Everything's on the right path.

Until I get to school.

I haven't even gotten to my locker when I hear an announcement come over the loudspeaker. "Will Kendall Williams please report to the main office, Kendall Williams to the main office."

Yikes. It's probably so they can schedule my detention for skipping class. But whatever. Detention isn't that bad. At least, not that I imagine. I've never actually been to detention. But I know you pretty much just sit in a room and do your homework.

I stop at my locker to drop my coat off and gather my books for the morning.

By the time I'm done, they've called me to the office two more times. God, don't they have anything else going on? It's that much of a slow day that they have to be that concerned with me and my stupid detention?

But when I get to the office, I find Brandon, Madison, and Micah sitting in the reception area, waiting for me.

"Finally," Micah says. "Where have you been, babe?"

"I was at my locker," I say. "Wait . . . what are you guys doing here?"

Madison doesn't answer me. She just taps her shoe on the floor and looks bored. "I hope this runs into first period," she says. "And they better give us a pass. I want to miss class, but if I'm late again, Mr. Turturo is going to flip."

"Mr. Jacobi called us down here," Brandon says.

"Oh." I sit down. "It must have something to do with tutoring."

Brandon shrugs, and I can tell we're wondering the same thing. Why would Mr. Jacobi call us down here about tutoring? He could just talk to us in class. You don't get called down to the main office unless you've done something wrong, unless you're in trouble for something. But we haven't done anything. We—

"There you are!" Mr. Jacobi says, hurrying into the main office. I wonder if he was at that coffee shop, grabbing coffee. He looks at us. "I have received some very disturbing news from Ms. Gruber, the elementary school teacher, about the methods that some of you are using to teach fractions."

Hmmm. I don't recall any crazy methods we used. Although, supposedly they're changing how they teach math, like, every year lately. So whatever we learned when we were in fourth grade is probably out of date. But how are we supposed to know that? It's not like they gave us any training.

"Does anyone want to explain themselves?" Mr. Jacobi asks. His eyes land on each one of us. Wow. I never realized how penetrating his stare is. "Anyone?"

No one says anything.

"Okay," he says. "Will this jog any memories?"

He rummages through his bag and produces a magazine. A magazine that he holds up and flutters around in front of him so hard that the secretary looks up from her computer.

"Hey!" Micah says. "That's the magazine we gave to that girl, uh, our student . . . What was her name?"

Oh my God. "Vivienne," I supply helpfully.

"Good job," Mr. Jacobi says sarcastically. "You can imagine my surprise when I found out that my students—who were supposed to be setting a shining example for those who are less fortunate—were bribing the young people!"

That doesn't really make any sense. Because Vivienne definitely wasn't less fortunate than us. She had a Michael Kors watch, for God's sake.

"Now," Mr. Jacobi says. "Which one of you came up with the bright idea to give this magazine to Vivienne?"

Everyone gets very quiet.

Micah looks down at the floor. Brandon just sits there, his hands folded in his lap. My hands tighten around the strap of my bag. Even Madison seems nervous.

I know we're all thinking the same thing—it was Madison's fault, but none of us are going to tell on her. It's one thing to get in trouble for something like this. It's another to actually squeal on someone.

"If none of you want to tell me which one of you came up with this idea, then I'm going to have to assume it was all of you."

Still no one says anything.

Great. Now I'm going to end up in detention again, probably for longer this time. I glance at Brandon out of the corner of my eye. Is it wrong that I'm kind of excited about the fact that we'll be in detention together? Not that we'll be able to talk, but still. Detention with Brandon seems dangerous and forbidden. Maybe he'll pass me a note when the teacher isn't looking. And then I'll smile and—

"Well, then I have no choice but to fail the four of you," Mr. Jacobi says.

"What?" I gasp. "*Fail* us?"

"Yes, Ms. Williams," Mr. Jacobi says. "This is a gross breach of an agreement we had with the elementary school, and all of you will have to pay for that."

"But that's not fair!" I say. "It's not our fault!"

"It *is* your fault," Mr. Jacobi says.

I glance at Madison. Surely she's going to step up and admit that she's the one who did it. But she's just sitting there, shaking her head with an outraged look on her face, like she can't believe this is happening to her.

And then I get it. She's waiting for someone else to take the blame.

Ha!

There's no way that's going to happen.

If I'm going to fail because of her, she's going to have to fail as well.

And then I see Brandon.

He's shaking his head, and I know what he's thinking. There goes his A.

But then why doesn't he tell on Madison? Is he going to? Maybe I should just tell Mr. Jacobi she's the one who did it.

But then I realize the problem with that plan. If I accuse Madison, she's going to accuse me back. And if she accuses me back, it's going to look like we're just doing it because we don't like each other. Mr. Jacobi knows that we got into a fight that day right before going into the school.

I look at Brandon again.

He looks miserable.

And then I know what I have to do.

"Mr. Jacobi," I say, standing up. "I'm the one who gave Vivienne the magazine."

Chapter 14

Okay, so it's not like I'm offering to fail math for a *boy*. It really isn't. I mean, let's face it. I have a chance of failing anyway, and Brandon really doesn't deserve to fail. In fact, it feels kind of noble, standing up and sacrificing myself for the cause.

It's like I'm in the last scene of a movie, where I've done something to prevent an injustice, and now I'm going to be led away all martyr-like to a jail cell. It almost feels like I should put my hands out and wait for Mr. Jacobi to slap on some handcuffs.

But before I have a chance to really bask in the glory of my sacrifice, Brandon speaks up.

"That's not true," he says. "It wasn't Kendall who gave Vivienne the magazine. It was Madison."

I gasp.

Madison gasps.

The only one who doesn't gasp is Micah. He just nods. "Yup," he says. "It was Madison."

"That's a lie!" Madison says. "Kendall admitted it. She's the one who gave Vivienne the magazine!"

"Oh, please," Brandon says. "You're the one who's into reading all that stuff."

He points to Madison's bag, which is on the floor. A bunch of magazines are poking out of the top.

"That doesn't prove anything!" Madison says.

We all start talking at once then, and Mr. Jacobi puts his hand up and shouts, "Enough!"

We all shut up.

"Kendall," he says, "is this true? Is Madison the one who gave Vivienne the magazine?"

I nod. Then I realize I'm still standing up, so I quickly sit down.

"Then why did you say you were the one who did it?" he asks.

"Because I didn't think it was fair that everyone got in trouble," I say. "Brandon has worked really hard for his grades."

Mr. Jacobi looks at me like he doesn't know if he should believe me or not. I hold my breath and keep his gaze, not daring to move. And then I see understanding dawn on his face. "Well," he says.

He turns to Micah. "You are corroborating this story?"

Micah nods.

And then a little evil grin comes over Mr. Jacobi's face. "Good," he says. "Ms. Baker, please come with me. The rest of you are free to go to class."

"But it's their word against mine!" Madison whines. "And you know that Kendall doesn't like me!"

"True." Mr. Jacobi steeples his fingers together. "But the young student in question told her teacher who gave her the magazine."

"So then why did you ask us?" Brandon asks. "If you already knew?"

"Because I wanted to see if you would admit it. But apparently some of you don't know how to do the right thing. Now please follow me to the principal's office, Madison."

It's such a dirty trick that I can't even muster up any kind of happiness that Madison is getting in trouble.

I sigh and pick my bag up, then head out of the office.

I'm halfway down the hall when I hear Brandon call my name.

"Kendall!"

I turn around to see him hurrying toward me. "Hey," he says.

"Hi."

He's so close that my heart does a little somersault, and it feels like butterflies are cartwheeling around in my stomach.

"That was really awesome, what you did back there," he says. "I wasn't . . . I want to let you know that I would never have let you take the blame."

"I know," I say. "Thanks. It means a lot, what you did."

He sighs and takes a deep breath. "I'm sorry, you know, for how things have been between us."

"It's not your fault." I give him a small smile, trying not to let him see how crazy I'm going inside, how I feel tingly all over, how much I miss him, how I want so badly to be back in his life, even if it's just as friends. "I know I dropped a lot on you with um . . . what I told you."

"And it's still true? What you said about my mom? About being able to see her?" He's looking at me, giving me a chance to say I made it up.

My throat gets tight, and my heart squeezes. It would be so easy to make up some kind of excuse. But I know I can't do that anymore.

"It's true," I say. "I know you don't understand it, but I don't . . . I don't want to lie to you, Brandon."

I expect him to brush by me down the hall, but to my surprise he doesn't. He just nods.

We stand there for a second, not saying anything. I'm trying to think if there's anything I can do to convince him, or if I should even bother. And then Mrs. Dunham appears down the hall. My heart soars. She's back, because I'm with Brandon! And if she's back, there might be a chance.

And seeing her gives me an idea.

"Brandon," I say. "I can't make you believe me, and I understand that you're doubtful. But I do see your mom." I take a deep breath. "She has long hair and she's wearing a flowing blouse and she really loves you a lot. And she told me about the green paper, the one she gave you right before she died."

A look of shock crosses over Brandon's face. "She told you about that?"

"Yes."

He sighs. "It just sounds so crazy, Kendall. You have to know that."

"I do know that."

He doesn't say anything, and I can't bear to just stand here. I won't be able to stand it if he walks away. So I decide to do it first. "Well, I'm always here if you want to talk. Take care of yourself, Brandon."

I turn and start to walk down the hall, my heart beating fast, my stomach in knots. I'm sad. But I'm also proud of myself for telling the truth.

"Kendall!" Brandon calls.

I turn around.

He rushes up to me. "Don't walk away yet." He bites his lip in frustration. "I don't know about this whole ghost thing. But I know you're a good person, Kendall."

I nod. I can feel my eyes filling up with tears. It means

so much to me that he said I'm a good person, that he at least isn't totally discounting what I'm saying.

He steps closer to me. "I'm sorry I left that day," he says. "When you told me. I was just shocked. And I'm still not sure I believe it, but I . . . I *miss* you, Kendall."

"I miss you, too," I breathe.

"Can we try again?" he asks. "To be boyfriend and girlfriend?"

"I want to," I say. "But what about the stuff with your mom?"

"I don't know," Brandon says. He looks down at the floor, and for a second I'm afraid he's going to take it all back. But then he looks up. "We'll just have to figure it out together."

I smile, and then he brushes his lips against mine.

And then he takes my hand and walks me to class.

Over the next week things start to get back to normal.

Brandon and I are together again. Ellie and I are friends again. (It feels a little weird that I haven't told her about the ghosts, especially since Brandon knows, but I'm planning on telling her soon. I just have to find the right time.)

It's a Wednesday afternoon after school, and Brandon's walking me home when my phone rings, displaying a number I don't recognize on the caller ID.

"Hello?" I say.

“Hi, Kendall?” a voice says. “It’s me.”

Even though I’ve never heard her voice on the phone before, I recognize it instantly. It’s my mom.

“Oh,” I say. “Um, hi.”

“Hi.”

There’s a pause.

“What are you doing?”

“I’m just walking home. With Brandon.”

Next to me Brandon smiles and squeezes my hand.

“Oh.” If she’s surprised I’m with Brandon, she doesn’t let it show in her voice. There’s a long pause, and I’m not sure if she’s waiting for me to say something or not. But she called me, so I’m not going to make an effort to make conversation. I stay quiet.

“Anyway,” she says. “I was just calling to let you know that I’m going to be in the area later, and I’d love to have dinner with you.”

I’m surprised by her offer, and confused. Do I really want to meet with her? I don’t know.

“Are you there?” she asks.

“Yes,” I say. “Um, can I text you in a little while? And let you know?”

“Of course.”

“Okay.”

“Okay.”

Another pause.

"Well, bye," she says.

"Bye."

I click off and stare at the phone.

"Who was that?" Brandon asks.

"My mom."

"Oh." He's surprised. Brandon knows I haven't seen my mom since I was little, but I haven't told him about the recent developments.

"I went to see her a couple of weeks ago," I say.

His eyes widen in surprise. "Wow," he says, and squeezes my hand. "How was that?"

I shrug. "It was okay." We're at my house now, but we stand on the porch, talking. I would invite Brandon inside, but my dad's truck is in the driveway, and I kind of want to talk to Brandon about this in private. "But now she wants to meet me for dinner tonight."

"And you don't want to go?"

I fiddle with the key chain on my backpack. "It's not that I don't want to go. It's that I don't *know* if I want to go."

He nods.

"It's just . . . I don't understand why she's suddenly so interested in seeing me. I mean, she didn't have any interest in getting in touch with me until I went and saw her."

"Maybe she was afraid."

"Afraid? Of what?"

"Rejection."

"Maybe." The thought never occurred to me before. That my mom might be afraid that if she tried to reach out to me, I would reject her. Of course, that doesn't explain why she left in the first place. But maybe she had reasons I can't even begin to understand. Kind of like how I had reasons for the crazy things I was doing and I couldn't tell anyone. "Anyway," I say. "I should probably go inside and start my homework. I'll call you later?"

"Yeah. And text me about what happens with your mom."

Brandon gives me a quick kiss, and then I walk inside.

I say hi to my dad, then grab a snack and start working on my homework.

But a second later he walks into the kitchen, where I'm sitting. "Everything okay?"

I'm about to answer automatically that it is, but then I change my mind. "Not really. Mom called me. She wants to meet for dinner."

My dad nods. "And do you want to go?"

"I don't know."

He nods again. "Well, it's your decision. You can do whatever you want, and I'll support you, as always. But if you do decide to go, I'll go with you if you want."

"To meet Mom?"

"Yeah." He must know what I'm thinking—that it would be awkward for him to be there while I'm having dinner with my mom—because he quickly adds, "I wouldn't go in or anything. But I could drive you, and then I could wait outside."

"You'd do that for me?"

"Of course," he says. "Whatever you need from me, Kendall, I'm here."

I think about it. "Okay," I say. "I think I'll go." I twist my hands. "But that doesn't mean I want to see her all the time or anything."

"Of course not," my dad says. "You'll take it one step at a time."

I text my mom a quick reply, accepting her invite and telling her the name of a restaurant on Main Street. That way, while we're eating, my dad can have stuff to do. He can hang out in the bookstore or browse around the hardware store.

A couple of hours later, when I'm done with my homework, my dad asks if I'm ready.

"I guess."

We drive to the restaurant, and on the way there we don't talk about anything serious. Instead, we talk about TV shows and joke around about how my dad likes a song by this new boy band. The ride is actually kind of nice. I'm still not sure I want to get into how I'm feeling or what it means that I'm doing this. I kind of just want to *feel* my feelings, instead of analyzing them. Which is totally weird, especially for me. Usually, I love to analyze.

When we pull up outside the restaurant, I can see my

mom through the window. She's sitting at a table, sipping a ginger ale and looking around anxiously.

"I'm nervous," I say out loud.

"You don't have to do this," my dad says. "It's not too late to change your mind."

And honestly, it's him saying that that makes me want to go. It's like it's going to be okay no matter what.

"No," I say, "I want to."

"Whatever happens in there, it doesn't change anything. You're still amazing."

"Thanks, Dad."

"You're welcome." He squeezes my hand. "Call me when you're done, okay?"

"Okay."

I hop out of the car, and then I watch as my dad pulls out and disappears down the street toward the shops.

I stand outside the restaurant for a moment, thinking about everything that's happened these past couple of months. My first boyfriend, my first breakup, my fight with Ellie, my mom coming back into my life . . .

The whole time, I kept thinking about what I could do to fix things, to make things better. What I didn't realize is that sometimes things don't always have to be black and white. They can be gray.

Brandon doesn't have to believe me about the ghosts, and he doesn't have to not believe me. My mom and I don't have to have a close relationship right off the bat, but I don't have to hate her either. I don't have to convince Mrs. Dunham's ghost that I'm right for her son—I just have to make sure I'm doing the best I can.

Because that's all any of us can do, really. Our best. And then hope it works out.

The snow is starting again, and flakes fall onto my fingers as I reach out and open the door to the restaurant.

But the warmth envelops me as soon as I walk in.

I stand there for a moment, just watching my mom, thinking about how much I really do look like her.

And then, after a second, I walk forward, into my future, ready for whatever it holds.

Sometimes a girl just needs a good book.
Lauren Barnholdt understands.

www.laurenbarnholdt.com

EBOOK EDITIONS ALSO AVAILABLE

From Aladdin M!X KIDS.SimonandSchuster.com

Real life. Real you.

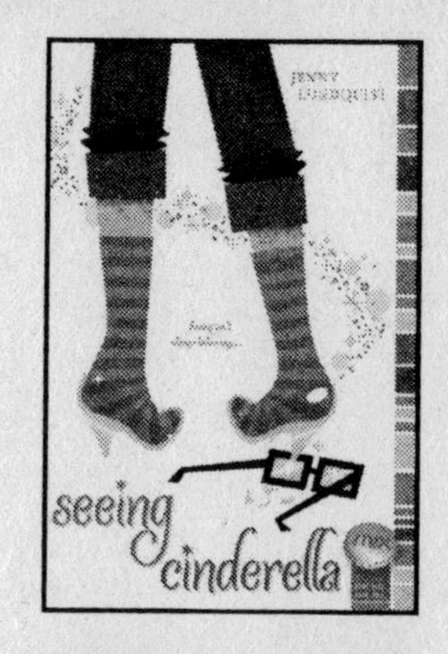

Don't miss any of these **terrific** Aladdin M!X books.

EBOOK EDITIONS ALSO AVAILABLE | KIDS.SimonandSchuster.com